✓ S0-BZU-587

"This isn't going to work, April," he said softly.

"I'm not Philip Marlowe, or Sam Spade, or Nick from Nick-and-Nora—"

"No, but you'll do." She pressed herself against his chest, her body as slight and sultry as a feminine whisper in a dark bedroom. He gritted his teeth and set her aside to open the door and shepherd her out.

"Maybe I should come back tomorrow…during business hours?" she suggested hopefully. "Maybe if I wore a snazzy tailored suit and a hat pulled down over one eye—?"

Oh, you crazy, mixed-up dame. "This isn't a Hollywood fantasy, April." He scowled, willing himself not to succumb to the lure of her jeweled eyes.

"Well, really!" April said loftily. She put her hands on her hips and spun around, sashaying down the hall toward the elevator, feathers bobbing, heels clicking, long, full tail sweeping the floor as it swung from side to side. "When you change your mind, you know where to find me."

"No, I don't," Tony said, involuntarily.

Saucily she glanced back over her shoulder. "You're an investigator, aren't you?" The elevator bell chimed, the doors slid open with a swoosh and she stepped inside. "So investigate."

Dear Reader,

You face the eternal question that has plagued womankind throughout the ages: you're trapped on a desert island with one man. You choose: (a) Sylvester Stallone (b) Daniel Day-Lewis or (c) Tom Hanks.

Upon serious reflection, you may consider: Sly might be able to tear down trees with his bare hands and strap together a raft out of jungle vines but you wonder—what are you going to talk about? Daniel will look really, really good and want to discuss deep, philosophical issues at great length but all you can think about is does he ever lighten up? If you pick Tom Hanks because he's smart and handsome and charming and *funny*—then have we got the books for you!

LOVE & LAUGHTER—a look at the lighter side of love. With our inspiration ranging from the beloved screwball comedies of yesterday to the romantic comedies of today, we searched high and low, far and wide, just about everywhere, in fact, for authors who love and write romance and comedy. The results, if we dare be so immodest, have been absolutely fabulous.

We are pleased to welcome longtime Loveswept author Judy Griffith Gill into the LOVE & LAUGHTER lineup. *There's Something About the Nanny*... combines all the best elements of romantic comedy with a little dash of magic. Carrie Alexander, a RITA nominee for Best First Book, harks back to the screwball comedies of yesterday in a delightful romp. April Pierce, *The Madcap Heiress*, will steal your hearts as quickly as she does the hero's!

With love—and laughter!

Malle Vallik

Malle Vallik
Associate Senior Editor

THE MADCAP HEIRESS
Carrie Alexander

Harlequin Books

TORONTO • NEW YORK • LONDON
AMSTERDAM • PARIS • SYDNEY • HAMBURG
STOCKHOLM • ATHENS • TOKYO • MILAN
MADRID • WARSAW • BUDAPEST • AUCKLAND

ISBN 0-373-44008-1

THE MADCAP HEIRESS

Copyright © 1996 by Carrie Antilla

Here I am, packing my possessions for a move, and there's no avoiding the obvious: I have too many books. Too many magazines, too many books, too many movies on video, too many books, too many files, scribbled notepapers, manuscripts...and did I mention the books? Way too many books.

My books and movies and magazines aren't just a hoard, though; they're inspiration...professional inspiration. *The Madcap Heiress,* for instance, was directly inspired by the wonderful, wacky, screwball comedies of the thirties and forties—movies like *Bringing Up Baby, My Man Godfrey, The Awful Truth, The Philadelphia Story.* The men are debonair, the women wear marabou, and witty repartee flies faster than a convertible with an heiress at the wheel. I love 'em. In fact, I had so much fun writing this rollicking romantic comedy that I couldn't stop. Look for my second LOVE & LAUGHTER book, *The Amorous Heiress,* in spring of 1997.

Maybe I was wrong. Maybe it isn't possible to have *too* many books. There's always a smidge of space up on the top shelf. *The Madcap Heiress* will fit if I squeeze...

—Carrie Alexander

1

A Damsel in Feathered Distress

FIFTEEN MINUTES into Tony Farentino's fledgling career as a private eye, he received his first client.

A peacock.

Since he'd discovered his uncle Rocco's bottom-drawer supply of hooch *two* minutes into his fledgling career as a private eye, perhaps the arrival of a five-foot iridescent-feathered peacock wasn't so shocking. While three shots of 80-proof whiskey on an empty stomach were liable to produce some pretty strange hallucinations in any man, they were especially lethal to one who'd recently returned from five months of deprivation at an archaeological excavation site in the jungles of Guatemala.

Tony put the Jim Beam back and shut the drawer. He used both hands to straighten his listing head. The peacock joggled back into focus.

"Farentino Investigations?" it asked.

"Yeah, but—"

"Are you hard-boiled?"

Tony blinked, taken aback. "Just half-crocked," he admitted. The peacock clucked, but nodded agreeably.

"Are you cynical and world-weary?" it chirped.

Tony reflected briefly. Considering that he'd just suffered an earthquake, the destruction of several months' work and, subsequently, a denial of tenure by the exclusive private college whose cushy ivy-covered environs had up to then willingly sheltered him between digs as long as he consented to teach a few classes now and then...

He took a deep breath and said, "Exceptionally so." Hence the Jim Beam.

The peacock—technically a peahen, Tony realized, staring at a pair of luscious legs displayed to perfection in sheer black turquoise-tinted hose—seemed to find this answer acceptable. A satisfied cooing sound issued from her puckered pink lips.

Her lively eyes sparkled. "Did you grow up as the oldest son in a rowdy Irish-Catholic family? And did you follow your gruff but lovable dad into the police force only to have your closer-than-a-brother partner shot dead before your eyes, making you pledge to hunt down his killer and issue .38-caliber justice even though you'd lose your badge? Did you wallow in a shady underworld of con men, gin joints and strippers with hearts of gold?" She waved extravagantly at the room, making her feathered bat-wing sleeves flap. "Does your job as a private eye just barely pay for your cigarettes and whiskey? Do you have a dingy office with flyspecked shades, an out-of-date calendar and a buxom secretary named Lola?"

"No."

"Whaddya mean 'no'?" she squeaked.

Tony shrugged. The peahen had only to look around her to see the answer to her last question. Due to Miss Estelle—who was as far from buxom floozyhood as was womanly possible—Rocco's office was the very model of humming efficiency. It was bright, clean, well furnished. The reception room boasted thriving plants that were fertilized on schedule once a month and a coffee table stacked with current magazines.

Though it was true that Tony was an oldest son, his heritage was Italian and Greek and his parents lived in Delaware with two of his four beautiful, sassy younger sisters. His various partnerships at archaeological sites around the globe had all gone smoothly; except for numerous inoculations, no one had ever been shot. Other than infrequent parking citations and the time that Uncle Rocco had made him buy tickets to the Policemen's Ball, he hadn't associated overmuch with either side of the law. He hadn't smoked since he was fourteen and experimenting. And the only thing the slightest bit sleazy private dickish about Farentino Investigations was the whiskey bottle in the bottom drawer, which, thanks to Tony's temporary wallow in world-weariness, was nearly empty.

"I meant just that," he said, and ticked his negative responses off on the fingers of his right hand. "No, no, no, no and, quite obviously, no."

"Oh, well," the birdwoman said with a sigh. Her expression wilted, then brightened considerably when her gaze lit on the shot glass he'd placed in the exact center of the desk blotter. "That's okay. You're hired anyway."

Beneath his deep tan Tony blanched, partly because of the roiling effect of the whiskey he'd chugged but mostly because he wasn't prepared to be hired—even by a peahen. Certainly not by one whose turquoise eyes were exotically enhanced with lines of smoky kohl, shadows of lime green and a sprinkling of golden specks—eyes sexy enough to make him wish to prostrate himself at her feet—her talons?—and pledge his eternal avian devotion.

Without waiting for an invitation, she gracefully moved to one of the chairs placed before the desk and sat, pushing aside the long fanned plumes of her trainlike tail. When she crossed her legs, Tony could have sworn her silk stockings whispered his name.

Chalk-mouthed, he stared bleakly into the empty carafe set on the corner of the desktop. He scrubbed one hand through his short black hair, fervently wishing Miss Estelle was on duty with her omniscient coffee-serving radar and her no-nonsense manner of dispatching unexpected visitors. She'd have taken care of the peacock before it could reach Rocco's inner sanctum, saving Tony from the trouble—and embarrassment—of explaining his distressing situation to a gaudy oversize bird with uncommonly arresting eyes and legs and . . . feathers.

"I can pay." She pulled a wadded envelope out of a tiny gold pouch strung on a cord around her waist.

Heaven forbid that a ladybird should flit around Chicago without a place to keep her lipstick, Tony thought. He squinted suspiciously as she placed the envelope on the desk. Actually, the way his life had been going lately, it seemed appropriately Felliniesque that he should be entertaining a petite woman dressed as a peafowl instead of scraping at thousand-year-old dirt under a steamy Guatemalan sun.

Sonova—*bird.* Had he come to this?

At least, come tomorrow morning, he'd be able to blame tonight's hallucination on those three shots of Jim Beam. Whereas the Cayaxechun earthquake had been all too real. And no one's fault at all.

No one's fault, he echoed sourly. Not a bad pun. See, already he could laugh about it!

Curious, he lifted the flap on the envelope. It was stuffed with crisp hundreds. "Is that enough for a down payment?" the peahen asked, her fluty voice both eager and earnest.

"It's more than enough for a retainer," he commented, and cleared his throat gruffly. He had to explain. Sooner would be better than later.

Instead Tony took the envelope and riffled through the bills like a cardsharp with a marked deck. It was a lot of money; he was sorely tempted. Although he'd made a good salary, for the past several years every spare dime had gone toward the Cayaxechun excavation. There'd always been some unexpectedly vital item the funding didn't cover and his team couldn't do without. Now the mortgage on his modest two-bedroom house in Wicker Park was coming due and since he was more or less out of a job...

Tony tossed the envelope back on the desk. If he actually took a job from a peacock Rocco would bust a gut laughing. And then he'd probably make Tony work the case just to teach him a lesson. "I'm afraid Farentino Investigations isn't accepting new clients for the time being, Miss—"

She regarded him levelly for a long second, then slowly blinked, flashing her gold-and-green lids and too-thick-to-be-real ebony lashes. "Pierce," she supplied, smiling sweetly. "April Pierce."

April Pierce.

"Ohhh," Tony said with a headachy groan. He'd been out of the city for five months and back for just two weeks but one had only to have picked up a newspaper to recognize the name. Capricious April Pierce was the current darling of the gossip columnists, a flibbertigibbet society princess without a care in the world or a serious thought in her head.

She was Chicago's very own madcap heiress.

And he was apparently a player in this evening's escapade.

April leaned forward, the lime green feathers on the backside of her loose sleeves and tight leotard rippling in fluid harmony. "You've heard of me?"

"Suddenly that ridiculous getup of yours is making a weird kind of madcap sense," Tony growled, trying to sound like the cynical P.I. she'd apparently been seeking.

"Oh, this." She shrugged in dismissal, the satiny turquoise fabric of her leotard glinting across the swells of her small, pert breasts. The attached hood clung sleekly to her head, concealing her hair and forming a deep widow's peak low on her forehead. "The gang's having a masquerade ball. We're on a scavenger hunt," she explained, withdrawing a tiny slip of paper from the gold pouch. She consulted it. "Would you happen to have a slice of Sacher torte or a key to an executive washroom? No? I thought not. You don't look like the executive type."

Which was neither here nor there, Tony thought grumpily. The "gang" must be the Palace Circle Pranksters, the rowdy group of socialites April led on a merry chase around the city in an ongoing, usually disruptive quest for excitement and amusement. The past Saturday night—technically Sunday morning—the whole lot of them had been arrested for hanging children's swings off the outdoor Picasso sculpture at the Daley Center. They'd spent several hours in the downtown lockup before someone's daddy had pulled strings at the mayor's office to get them pardoned en masse.

"So you decided to stop by in the middle of your party to hire a private investigator?" he scoffed. "Gimme a break, lady. I'm not that gullible."

Frostily April tilted up her small pointed chin. "I was on the way to the brokerage firm on the fifteenth floor."

"It's quarter to ten on a Wednesday night," he pointed out. *Crazy dame.* "Them ain't regular business hours." For some reason, he felt oddly pleased with himself. This investigatory stuff was getting easier all the time. Maybe he should quit the archaeology racket for good and concentrate on developing what was clearly a natural talent for another kind of snooping. Especially since he was already lapsing into the appropriate vernacular.

"Silly man. No one would stage a masquerade ball during regular business hours. What happened was that Ju-Ju called her stepsister who is having an affair with one of the brokers to get the security code so I could slip in and borrow the key to the executive washroom that's fifth

on our list. It's worth twenty-five points to my team.''
April smiled knowingly despite the garbled explanation.
''Winning a scavenger hunt is all about having the right
connections.''

''Which you have, I hear. In adorably madcap excess.''

Her vivid eyes darkened at his sarcastic tone. ''Is there
something wrong with that?''

''Not to them that's got it.'' Tony knew he was being
needlessly rough on her. No fault to frilly, fluffy, little
April Pierce that the tenured position that should have
been his had instead been awarded to a mealymouthed
second-rate epigraphist with connections up the wazoo.

She faltered. ''I—I don't know what to say.''

''Forget it.''

''Forget what?''

Tony cracked a smile. ''Very good.''

''No, I mean it. Forget what, exactly?''

He rose from Rocco's swivel chair and circled the desk.
April popped up with a fluttering of various feathered
parts. She really was quite an alluring bird, as aglitter and
aglow as the emperor's faux nightingale, tiny, delicate,
silkily garbed, but kind of gutsy and intrepid, too. If he'd
been a licensed investigator he might have taken her
case—if it *was* a case and not a joke, which was a mighty
gigantic if—for the promise of its sheer entertainment
value.

But he wasn't, Tony reminded himself. For the next two
weeks, he was Rocco's glorified caretaker, nothing more.
Farentino Investigations was just a port in the storm. Or,
so to speak, a stronghold in an earthquake. April Peacock would be an unnecessary distraction as he licked his
wounds and tried to decide what to do with the rest of his
life.

''I repeat, Miss Pierce, we have no time for new clients
at the moment. Go check out the Yellow Pages for an

agency desperate enough to indulge your shenanigans, why don't you?"

She crossed her arms and tapped one slender, irritated, high-heeled foot. Her expression was haughty, her nostrils flared. "Well, really!"

Her plummy accent sounded as arch as that of every snobbish blue blood he'd ever met, but something about April's manner kept Tony from dismissing her out of hand. It might have been the hint of self-mockery hovering around her pursed lips. More likely it was the intriguing depth of emotion in her turquoise eyes—just discernible if one cared to look closely instead of taking her at frivolous face value.

Tony found that he did care to look. Extremely closely.

April cocked her head, batting her thick eyelashes. "Hmm, well, *really . . .*" she cooed seductively. She petted her palm across his biceps, then walked her fingers up his shoulder.

Despite the ticklish warmth that curled through him in response to her teasing touch, Tony withdrew. There was a false note about the peahen's flirtation. She was . . . hell, she was toying with him!

He waved his finger at her. "Uh-uh-uh, little girl."

April stamped her foot. She tossed her head. She crossed her arms beneath her breasts and pouted impressively.

Tony pointed to the door. "Take your pretty little feathered tail out of here, Miss Pierce. Farentino Investigations is a serious place of business, not an amusement park."

"I've got a serious problem," she insisted. "An honest-to-goodness, serious case for you to solve. Maybe even life-and-death!"

"Yeah, sure. Tell it to the Chicago PD."

She bit her lip, looking doubtful, then burst out with a fervent "But, Mr. Farentino! Dunky's missing!"

The pain in Tony's head pounded alarmingly at the inside of his skull. "Okay, that does it." He put his hands on the pain outside his head and pushed her toward the door that opened into the reception area. "You and your imaginary menagerie are out of here."

"My what?" she protested with a gulped laugh, digging in her heels but nonetheless skidding across the carpeted floor under Tony's single-minded propulsion. "My imagery—imenager—menaginary—" She untwisted her tongue to giggle infectiously.

Tony found himself smiling. "Peacocks. Donkeys. It's all the same to me." April was no longer resisting, so he took her hand and led her to the outer door that was inscribed with the agency name. The one he'd foolishly left unlocked.

"Really, there aren't any donkeys involved," she pleaded in a last-ditch effort. "It's my friend *Dunky*. Darryl Dunkington. He's been missing for over eighty-two hours now, ever since we got out of jail after the—" Obviously realizing that such details didn't lend her story any credence, she instead resorted to staring up at Tony with wide, frightened eyes. She enfolded his hand between hers and clutched it to her chest.

Again, he felt both a strong pull toward her and the opposing, nagging doubt that she was not being entirely honest. Her eyes were overly beseeching, her grip on his hand too showy, as though she was thoroughly reveling in her damsel-in-distress masquerade. He, however, was not the hard-boiled but honorable detective she'd expected. And there was no way he'd willingly put himself at the beck and call of a silly socialite's whimsy.

The Dunkington name did sound vaguely familiar. Tony's curiosity flared; he extinguished it. Likewise, he ruthlessly squelched any inklings of sympathy April's plea had generated.

Ridding himself of the accompanying physical attraction might take some doing, though, he decided as his fingertips slid of their own volition across the satiny curve of April's left breast. Her heartbeat thudded beneath his palm, seeming as frantic and close to the surface as a wild bird's. Which couldn't be part of her act, could it?

"This isn't going to work, April," he said softly.

Her mouth curved. "Are you sure?"

"I'm not Philip Marlowe, or Sam Spade, or Nick Whomever from Nick and Nora—"

"No, but you'll do." She pressed closer, her body as slight and sultry as a feminine whisper in a dark bedroom. Tony's left hand reached for her waist. She cooed something about how much she appreciated his help and rested her cheek on his chest. The peacock plumes rising up the back of her hooded head tickled his chin, making him want to laugh out loud even though, strangely enough, there was nothing funny about holding a woman-size peacock in his arms. By all rights it should have been hilarious.

"I mean it, April. I can't take this job."

Although he could easily convince her if he confessed to being not only an untrained P.I. but an incompetent archaeologist, too, he wasn't eager to look like that much of a fool. It might be nice to come out of this oddball encounter with a shred of dignity.

Tony gritted his teeth and set April aside so he could open the door. He shepherded her through it. "Maybe I should come back tomorrow...?" she suggested hopefully. "During regular business hours, if it means that much to you."

"Don't bother."

"Maybe if I wore a snazzy tailored suit and a hat pulled down over one eye—"

Oh, you crazy, mixed-up dame. "This isn't a Technicolor Hollywood fantasy, April, or a forties' black-and-white film noir." He put his hands in the pockets of his sun-bleached jeans, scowling as he willed himself not to succumb to the lure of her jeweled eyes. "This is real life, and if your friend Donkey is actually missing you'd be much better off telling it to the police."

"They think I'm a ditz."

Tony gave her peacock outfit the once-over. "I wonder why."

"Well, really!" April said loftily. She stuck her chin up in the air and challenged him with a glare, obviously expecting him to capitulate—to the money, if not to her charms. Wasn't that the way rich people operated?

When he remained stoic, she put her hands on her hips and spun around, sashaying down the hall toward the elevator, feathers bobbing, heels clicking, long, full tail sweeping the floor as it swung from side to side. "When you change your mind, you know where to find me."

"No, I don't," Tony said—involuntarily, or so he thought.

Saucily she glanced back over her shoulder. "You're an investigator, aren't you?" The elevator bell chimed, the doors slid open with a shwoosh, and she stepped inside. "So investigate."

"YOU'LL NEVER GUESS what I just saw," Rocco Farentino said, entering the reception area ten minutes later with a large paper bag from Clint Wong Foo's House of Imperial Delight. He was in his late fifties, a broad, muscular man thickening into fat, dressed in another of the expensive tailored suits that turned into an ill-fitting mass of wrinkles the instant he put them on.

A retired cop, Rocco favored cigars, gambling and showgirls. Also mixed drinks featuring rum-and-anything-but-a-paper-umbrella and beach volleyball played by women in string bikinis. If Miss Estelle hadn't superglued herself to the firm's computer, he would have gone for the buxom secretary named Lola. All in all, he fit April Pierce's image of a gumshoe much better than his nephew.

"I wouldn't make book on that if I were you," Tony said as he preceded Rocco into the inner office. His 80-proof headache had subsided to a dull ache. Hopefully Wong Foo didn't use MSG.

"You saw 'em, too?" Rocco pulled a wad of paper napkins from the top of the bag and threw them on the desk. Right on top of April's envelope of cash.

Tony's eyes narrowed. So that was why she'd been so sure she'd see him again...

He lifted tubs of wonton and shark's fin soup out of the bag and busily redistributed the napkins, taking the opportunity to slide April's retainer into his back pocket. If he returned the money tomorrow, Rocco would never have to know that his nephew's first client—nonclient, Tony amended determinedly—had been a peacock.

"Skipping down the sidewalk with open bottles of champagne, bold as can be." Rocco shook his head. "Though I wouldn't mind meeting up with the little glittery one again." He pried off a lid and rubbed his hands over the soup's peppery steam. "She was fine."

"There were two of them?" A crisp spring roll fell from Tony's chopsticks and rolled between the white cartons. "I only saw the one."

"Hell's bells, Tony, there was a whole party of 'em. Pirates, princesses, Klingons, a Bob Dole and a Hillary. It was the sexy little belly dancer who caught my eye." Rocco chuckled. "She jiggled and jangled when she walked—I'da liked to see her when she danced."

Tony chased the spring roll across the blotter, then resorted to stabbing it with a chopstick. "It was a masquerade party, I gather."

Rocco guffawed through a mouthful of dumpling, spraying bits of pork and fried batter. "Damn good observation technique, boy. I'll make an investigator of you yet!''

Tony wiped the flecks off his cheek and edged his chair farther away from the desk. "Now hold on, Uncle Rocco. I agreed to play the nominal figurehead of Farentino Investigations so you wouldn't have to shut down the office while you went on vacation. I don't remember saying anything about making the position permanent."

"Didn't that fancy college kick you out on your keister?"

Tony winced. "One could put it that way."

"I already did." Rocco looked smug. "So the upshot is that you need a job and I need an assistant." He scooped up a clump of lo mein noodles and munched happily. "Hang around the office for the next two weeks like we agreed. Give the place a chance." He snorted. "Miss Estelle won't let you get into anything you can't handle, believe you me!"

Tony grabbed the last moo shu chicken pancake before it fell prey to his uncle's wandering chopsticks and settled back in his chair. He had no problem sticking to the agreement. There were worse things than spending two uneventful weeks in a clean and pleasant office run by Miss Estelle. She was the kind of unobtrusive secretary who anticipated and catered to her boss's every need. He'd even receive a salary, one admittedly as nominal as his position, but what else could a walking disaster expect?

According to Rocco, the job would be a snap. All Tony had to do was hand out a few financial reports that Miss Estelle would complete and brief him on, and maybe ask a question or two of the occasional walk-in client prescreened by Miss Estelle. She would discreetly take down the details and do any mundane computer data base searches required, leaving the actual fieldwork for Rocco's return. Important or tricky investigations had been cleared off the agency's calendar.

Tony lifted a bite of pancake, dripping hoisin sauce, to his mouth. It was a job description he could handle. Mind you, not one word had been said about how to handle walk-in peacocks...

"Miss Estelle will show you anything you need to know before I get back," Rocco continued complacently. "That woman is an automaton." He burped as he hefted himself out of the chair to peer into the paper bag. "Damned if I didn't forget to uncork the liquid refreshments." He set several Tsing Tao Chinese beers on the desk and wandered out to rummage in Miss Estelle's desk for a bottle opener.

Feeling a yen to count hundred-dollar bills, Tony retrieved April's envelope from his back pocket. It was disconcerting to realize that Rocco expected Miss Estelle to baby-sit him for the next two weeks. Surely he could manage to return this money—an impressive four thousand bucks—on his own. Even a fledgling detective should be able to discover April Pierce's address. A figurehead detective, that was.

Rocco came back with a device that contained every gadget known to man. After a few false starts—corkscrew, putty knife, buttonhook—he finally unfolded the bottle opener and pried the caps off the beers. Tony watched, thinking that April Pierce's idealized version of a private eye doubtlessly would have opened the bottles with his teeth. He probably would've taken hold of any madcap heiresses in the vicinity, bent 'em back over his arm and kissed 'em senseless, too.

There was something to be said for April's version.

As Tony surreptitiously returned the packet of money to his jeans, his glance fell on a stray peacock feather lying under the desk. Since Rocco was thoroughly absorbed in crunching, smacking and slurping, Tony made a quick retrieval. Mulling over his situation, he absently brushed the feather back and forth across his palm until the downy barbs had aroused his nerve endings to the point where his hand literally itched to grasp and caress something a bit more substantial. Like the one and only madcap heiress herself.

The feather's "eye" winked up at him as he fiddled with it, rolling it between his thumb and index finger. The pupil was a dark blue, rimmed by a turquoise iris, framed in circles of gold and lime green—not unlike his memory of April's slanted eyes. For a flibbertigibbet princess, she had some kind of staying power.

Regretting the distraction, wanting to rid himself of it—her—Tony shook his head and blew out a deep breath like a Thoroughbred after a hard race.

Rocco looked up from scraping his chopsticks at the bottom of a carton. "Hope you didn't want any more of the orange-flavored beef. I just finished it." He chewed, swallowed, grinned. "There's still plenty of pea pods."

"I'll take a fortune cookie." Tony checked his watch, then broke the cookie in half and took out the fortune. "We'd better leave soon for O'Hare."

"Don't wanna miss that red-eye to Vegas," Rocco agreed. He was going to spend the first week of his vacation gambling and the second relaxing as either a pauper or a king at a prepaid Mexican singles' resort.

Tony nodded absently as he unfolded the slip of paper. He read the fortune. He looked at the peacock feather. His mind reeled. His stomach churned. His heart clutched. It isn't often that dessert provides both an insight into the future and a vital organ checkup.

"What's it say?" Rocco asked, scooping the remains of a half-demolished dumpling into his mouth.

Tony tried to laugh but groaned instead. The feather slipped through his fingers and wafted to the floor, where its garish eye stared up at him balefully.

"'All eyes are upon you,'" Tony quoted.

"Not a good omen for a private dick," Rocco said with another booming guffaw.

This time, Tony remembered to duck.

The Gamut of Butlers

2

A Gamut of Butlers

OF COURSE, it was obvious to everyone but Rocco Farentino that Miss Estelle was in love with him. What wasn't as obvious, at least to everyone but Miss Estelle, was that Rocco loved her in return.

Miss Estelle had waited three years for Rocco to recognize his feelings for her. If need be, she was prepared to wait three more.

Miss Estelle was an extremely patient woman.

She'd also had the foresight to make herself indispensable to Farentino Investigations. If, for some insane reason—a robust Miss 36 Double-D hovered at the edge of Miss Estelle's consciousness—Rocco foolishly attempted to rid himself of her admirable and unlimited skills, harsh reality and two tons of paperwork would collapse upon him like the Berlin Wall. Miss Estelle figured that once she had Rocco on his knees begging her return, the true negotiations could begin.

Not that Miss Estelle was a vindictive woman. She simply knew her strength: she ran the business, the secretarial swivel chair being the true seat of power at Farentino Investigations. And she knew her weakness: one hundred pounds dripping wet and she didn't wiggle when she walked. Not an atypical distribution of favors, from what Miss Estelle had observed in her forty-seven very perceptive years, but fortunately she had the brains to make the most of what she'd been given.

Ultimately Miss Estelle was certain she would triumph.

In the meantime, she would attend to the minor annoyance of Rocco's nephew's presence. With luck, Tony Farentino would be simply a blip in her radar screen. A gnat in her rarified airspace. Another bump in her Rocco road to romance.

She wanted him out of her office in two weeks. Maybe less.

None of these thoughts showed on Miss Estelle's narrow, pale face. She was sitting at the computer, bland as ever, fingers flying over the keyboard, when Tony looked around the doorjamb.

"Er...Miss Estelle?"

She blinked but didn't stop typing. "Yes, Mr. Farentino?"

"Just how would I go about finding a person's home address?"

"Is this regarding an ongoing case?"

Tony shook his head emphatically. "No, absolutely not. No. Not a case, certainly not a case, Miss Estelle, I assure you, no." He resisted the urge to wipe sweat from his brow.

Miss Estelle's meager eyebrows crept up her forehead. "Whatever you say, Mr. Farentino. One moment, please." She efficiently completed the last lines of an employee's background report for Em-Tee Tech Industries, a client she'd recruited by working her sources in the vast underground secretarial network, and exited the file. Several more keystrokes and she was ready. "Name?"

"Uh..." Tony had been staring off into space, wondering what had become of the peacock feather after he'd driven Rocco to the airport. It had vanished, along with the remains of their Chinese takeout. The superefficient Miss Estelle had struck, to be sure.

"The name, please."

Tony pulled himself together. Rocco's secretary waited, straight and square and spare, floating undisturbed within her self-contained world of limitless patience. He thought her rather eerie. "April Pierce."

Miss Estelle typed briefly, stopped with one finger poised, said, "I take it you don't have a license plate number?" and hit Enter before Tony could suggest she try Madcap.

Data flashed across the screen, but when Tony leaned closer to get a look, she quickly cleared the monitor. "It's 7600 Palace Circle," she said, her tone detached but clipped. "Chicago, Illinois."

Some great detective, Tony thought glumly. There he had a clue like "The Palace Circle Pranksters" sticking to his gumshoe and he'd still gone to Miss Estelle.

Since Tony was still hanging over her desk, she elaborated from photographic memory. "Town house purchased for 1.75 million, January last. No mortgage outstanding. Five-two, hazel/blond, D.O.B. 4/16/70. Unmarried. Quite a large number of traffic tickets. Will there be anything else, Mr. Farentino?"

"No, thanks, Miss Estelle." Assuming it was April and not her house who was five-two and hazel/blond, Tony worked out her age. Recently turned twenty-six? He'd thought she was barely legal. Living life as a madcap heiress must keep one young.

He went to the door, opened it and glanced back at Miss Estelle. "I'm heading out for a while..."

She consulted her immaculate daybook and pinned him in the doorway with a gimlet-eyed stare. "You have a late-afternoon appointment at Em-Tee Tech. I've just finished their report."

"Yes, Miss Estelle." Tony inched into the hallway, guiltily fingering the envelope of money tucked in the inside pocket of his black suede vest. Something about Uncle Rocco's secretary put him on edge. Probably her She Who Must Be Obeyed coffee mug. And matching attitude.

Her face remained impassive. "Four o'clock, Mr. Farentino." The "on the dot" was only implied.

"I'll be back in plenty of time."

"Very well, Mr. Farentino."

Tony shuffled his feet. "This is just a personal errand," he heard himself explaining. The secretary might well be reporting back to Rocco. "Not a case."

"As you say, Mr. Farentino."

"Okay, g'bye, then." The door clicked shut behind him.

"Good day, Mr. Farentino." Miss Estelle allowed herself a small shake of her head. Something about Rocco's nephew had momentarily disturbed her usually inviolable equilibrium.

It was probably nothing, she decided, making a note of April Pierce's name and address and tucking it into the file folder that already contained the peacock feather. She'd yet to meet a man she couldn't control.

Then again, Rocco *was* in Las Vegas, the quickie marriage capital of the world. Without her.

And with hundreds of 36 Double-D showgirls.

One of Miss Estelle's eyelids twitched.

PALACE CIRCLE, an offshoot of Lake Shore Drive, was an exclusive cul-de-sac of town houses and small mansions with stunning Lake Michigan views. Tony didn't have to search out house numbers to identify which one was April's. Only a madcap heiress could get away with lampposts striped like candy canes.

Her town house was dignified despite such whimsical touches. Tall and relatively narrow, it was constructed of massive blocks of silvery limestone, the facade ornamented with an artisan's oeuvre of carved details. There was a mansard roof, several tall chimneys, even flying buttresses chiseled into the shape of trumpeting angels.

The Gothic wrought-iron front gate opened with a creak. Tony mounted the broad front steps. They were crowded with an unmatched assortment of urns, amphorae and jardinieres planted with mounds of circusy petunias striped red and white, red and yellow, yellow and purple, pink and white. Two large gray stone lions guarded the front door. Winged lions with birdlike heads—gryphons, Tony remembered. The one on the left wore a jaunty beret and a crimson Harvard scarf. The one on the right sported a rhinestone diadem and bright pink nail polish on its three-inch-long claws.

Twenty-*six?* Tony wondered. April Pierce had to be a clear-cut case of arrested development. Well, only in some ways, he corrected, recalling her more, uh, womanly developments.

There was no obvious theme to the architectural style— the ten-foot-high double doors had been carved with gamboling satyrs, curling leafy tendrils, overflowing cornucopias and smiling maidens whose diaphanous gowns bared their plump, bouncing bosoms. Tony twirled the old-fashioned doorbell. And waited.

Several minutes later, he cranked it again, long and loud and impatiently. Though he pressed his ear to a bouncing bosom, the slab of mahogany was too thick for him to hear anything inside.

Tony had given up and was halfway down the steps when the door was opened by a shirtless bald hulk in a wide leather weight-lifting belt, striped gym shorts and biker boots. His pumped-up muscles gleamed with perspiration. The skin on his scowling face looked as if it had been mangled by an eggbeater.

"So whadja want?" The behemoth's voice rumbled like a cement mixer, but his accent was surprisingly British.

Miss Estelle had said April was single. Which didn't mean she couldn't have lovers. Tony swallowed. There was no telling what madcap heiresses went in for these days. A brief image of the fragile April tucked underneath the yards of muscled bulk on the doorstep cut into his heart, slicing to ribbons any vague hopes he'd had for... whatever.

"I'm looking for April Pierce," he said finally.

"Still in bed."

Hmm. Tony approached the door and found that he was, at six feet even, only an inch or two shorter than the hulk. Although he was sturdy enough himself, he was still about fifty—make that seventy-five—pounds lighter. Mr. Muscle crossed his arms and his assorted tattoos bulged. His deep-set eyes glinted in the shadow cast by his Neanderthal brow.

"Whatcha want April for?"

"It's business. My name's Tony Farentino. I think she'll see me."

The hulk grunted. "I took her breakfast tray up fifteen minutes ago." He went back inside, leaving the door open.

Breakfast tray? Tony blinked and followed. Breakfast tray. Now that might put a different spin on things.

The foyer looked like the inside of a music box. There was a settee with pink velvet upholstery, a gold Chippendale mirror, a gilt-and-ivory console, swirly pink marble floor and, twenty-five feet overhead, a vaulted ceiling with gold-leaf decoration.

"Wait in the salon." The hulk clumped up the marble staircase, the silver chains on his black leather boots jingling.

A butler? Tony wondered, dumbfounded, but beginning to smile. A cook? A houseboy? A general all-round tattooed muscle-bound dogsbody?

Every madcap heiress should have one.

The salon was on the right, featuring plush pink velvet sofas, rose moiré-satin drapes and an elaborate chandelier with dangling faceted teardrops. It looked like the inside of a jewelry box. Before Tony could sit, the hulk clumped back downstairs, frowning ferociously beneath the thick black unibrow bisecting his gnarled forehead. "She says you can go up," growled the limey cement mixer, and then he clumped away to the back of the house.

"Okay," Tony said to the empty salon. So the butler wasn't big on the niceties. "I'll go up." Just to return the money. Really.

The house was narrow but deep. The stairway spiraled back toward the front, disgorging Tony at a wide landing where mullioned windows framed the lake view. Sailboats dotted the water; the waves sparkled with sunshine.

He walked along the gallery, eyeing the white marble statuary tucked into various niches, and peeked past the first door he came to that was ajar. It opened into an expansive bedroom and there, ensconced within a meringue of sheer, draped, ruffled fabrics and tasseled pillows, on an opulent four-poster on a dais, was April Pierce.

She was occupied with her breakfast tray, which gave him a moment to stare unabashedly. Except for the greediness of her absorption with the jam pot, she looked like a cosseted china doll. He guessed that the heap of blush pink chiffon ruffles covering her was a bed jacket. Her wavy, jaw-length hair, the buttery blond of sunlight, was caught up in a wide pink grosgrain bow. Her skin seemed almost translucent; he wondered if it was the brilliance of her turquoise irises that showed through as a faint blue shadow on her lowered eyelids.

Tony's throat grew tight, his tongue felt heavy and thick. He suppressed an out-of-character urge to launch himself at the bed and mess things up a bit. He had to remember he was a methodical, by-the-book archaeologist type, not a rough-and-tumble private eye. He wasn't here for personal reasons. Blast it, anyway.

April popped a bite of flaky croissant in her mouth, glanced up and saw him. Her smile was sticky-sweet with strawberry preserves. "Come in, darling Mr. Farentino. I knew I could count on you to find me!" She waved him over, her fingertips shining with butter. "Breakfast?" she asked, daintily plucking a linen napkin from the tray.

Tony approached the dais, feeling like a serf genuflecting before royalty. "I've had breakfast, thank you. I stopped on the way over and even had lunch."

"Just another dreary early riser." April sighed. "How very predictable."

"Some of us have to work for a living."

She smiled around the beveled crystal lip of her glass of pale orange mimosa. "Oh, kind sir, you underestimate me." She set the goblet down and pushed the tray aside, then stretched luxuriously, her legs moving beneath the reembroidered lace coverlet drawn up to her waist. "Madcap heiressing is *very* hard work," she purred.

Tony couldn't help but smile, watching her. She was so irrepressibly decadent. "But someone's got to do it, right?"

"Exactly." She patted the bed. "Come sit down and we'll discuss the case."

Hesitating, Tony glanced around the room, taking in the polished black stone fireplace, the cream silk walls and antique lace at the windows, the extravagant arrangements of fresh flowers on every available surface. From the look of things, the cash in the envelope was just enough to buy April Pierce another amusing knick-knack. Would it be so wrong of him to consider taking this job? If he sort of explained his position to her and she still wanted to hire him?

He stepped up onto the carpeted platform and forced himself to say, "I really just came by to return your money."

April flounced. "No, please don't do that! Dunky needs you." She fluttered her long blond lashes. "*I* need you, Mr. Farentino."

"Maybe you'd better call me Tony." He brushed back the drifts of silky white stuff that were draped across the sleek black frame of the four-poster and sat at its foot.

April tossed aside some of the plump cushions and crawled forward on her hands and knees. Her blond head was nestled within the high ruffled collar of the bed jacket like a honeybee tucked into a blowsy pink camellia. "And I shall be known as Lola!"

Tony gaped at her. "What?"

"My assumed name for our undercover work," she explained matter-of-factly. She sat beside him with her legs folded under her, bouncing lightly on the springy mattress. "Oh, Tony, we'll have such fun." She clasped her hands under her chin with girlish delight. "Let's begin immediately."

"Whoa, slow down, April. I never said—"

"I last spoke to Dunky at brunch after we got out of jail Sunday morning. He had a teensy hangover and he swore he was going straight home afterward, but Talon says she hasn't seen him since. Of course, knowing Talon, that means practically zilch. She's not exactly the brother's-keeper type."

Tony sighed. "Talon is Donkey's sister?"

"Talon Dunkington. She owns a trendy River North art gallery. I wonder..." April tipped her chin up thoughtfully, then shook her head. "No, we should start at Windenhall."

"Windenhall?"

"The Dunkington estate. I can get us in to search Dunky's rooms."

"Now wait a minute. *We* are not doing anything, April. I'm not even sure that *I* am, but if I do, I'm going to do it alone." Tony took her by the shoulders and gave her a little shake. "Do you hear?"

She gazed meltingly into his eyes. "Gosh, you're so adorable I could just eat you up."

"Sheesh." He stared back. Was she that naive? Didn't she know enough not to say such provocative things while entertaining a man in her bedroom? Especially when the man concerned has just returned from five chaste months in a remote rain forest where the only female around had been Peggy Sue Burnside, a fifty-year-old geologist who preferred to converse with rocks?

Tony's gaze dropped to the pink velvet rosebud that was April's mouth. Damn, but he wanted to kiss her. He also wanted, with an ache that was really starting to get to him, to throw her back on the bed and part her ruffles like Moses parting the Red Sea.

Instead he snatched his hands away, holding them up blamelessly—or defensively—as he slid off the bed and backed down the dais. "You are nuts, lady. Certifiably nuts."

"I know. And isn't it fun?" With a chortle of pure pleasure April bounced off the bed and pranced across the room, shedding the bed jacket as she went. Underneath she wore a matching chiffon nightgown, layered from neck to toe with more of the semitransparent ruffles. Her figure made a slender, swaying silhouette beneath the rustling fabric as she stepped behind a gold-on-cream jacquard folding screen framed in art deco black lacquer.

A few seconds later she tossed the frothy gown over the top.

Tony dropped onto a padded bench at the foot of the dais. "I'm leaving, April," he said. "I'm outta here." But he didn't move. In fact, he couldn't even bring himself to look away.

"You can't get into Windenhall without me." Her fingers appeared, gripping the top of the screen, and she did something that made the whole shebang shimmy. Tony couldn't imagine what. No, actually, he could, and that was part of his problem.

"Also," April continued, her bottom pressing against the jacquard, making an enticing bump on Tony's side that widened his eyes to half-dollar size, "I'm the only one who can identify the thugs."

Her bottom was so taut and tidy he thought he could probably manage to hold it in one hand—with a bit of squeezing. He was drifting into fantasizing a situation where he could apply the theory when her words hit him.

Thugs? There were thugs?

"April?" he called, trying to sound casual even though his breath had seized up in his chest. "Did you say... 'thugs'?"

She stood on her toes to peek over the top of the screen. "They're looking for Dunky, too."

Tony exhaled. "So that means they're not behind his disappearance."

"Well, I don't know that for sure. I haven't actually seen them since we were all at the jailhouse together. The police had overreacted to the Pranksters' stunt with the swings and the Picasso, and by coincidence, the thugs had been arrested in some sort of brawl, which was awfully bad luck for Dunky since they'd been hunting for him. The good luck was that the thugs were in shackles. Still, Dunky was really scared. He turned as white as one of his blank canvases."

"Great," Tony muttered. "There are thugs." Now he couldn't quit the case even if he wanted to. There was no telling what a woman as heedless as April would get into on her own, and what with *thugs* hanging around...

Someone had to protect her.

And it looked as if he'd been elected, at least until he thought of a way out of it. Or until he delivered her into the lap of the police.

"I have an idea," April said lightly, apparently not bothered by the thought of thugs.

"Forget about your screwy ideas, please, at least for the moment. Tell me what the thugs looked like."

"Oh, one was huge, with lots of overdone muscles and a hatchet face. Real thuggish, y'know?" She opened a door behind the screen and Tony heard running water and the sound of toothbrushing. "The other was smaller. A sleazy type with a scar on his upper lip. Oily hair slicked back from a pasty white forehead."

Tony frowned. It sounded as though she'd watched the late, late show one time too many. He wondered if the thugs actually existed. This could all be a game—sort of like last night's scavenger hunt.

"What do these alleged thugs wa—" April came out from behind the screen and Tony choked on the rest of his words. She'd put on a sleeveless minidress so tight she looked as if she'd been shrink-wrapped, and thigh-high white lace stockings with over-the-knee electric blue boots. Her eyes seemed more blue than turquoise today, but that might have been because of the robin's-egg shade of her dress. She ran her fingers through the ruffled cap of her blond hair. "You like?"

He closed his eyes and prayed for the strength to resist. "Very nice," he said through gritted teeth, and forced his thoughts to return to the case. Keeping his eyes closed made that a lot easier. "What do the thugs want with Donkey, April?"

"You met my man, Godfrey," she said, which certainly didn't answer his question.

His eyes flashed open. "The bald hulk's name is Godfrey?"

April sashayed over to him and leaned down to whisper in his ear. "I wouldn't say that word around Godfrey if I were you. He doesn't know he's *b-a-l-d*."

The dress was too tight to gape, but it was scoop-necked and gave him a glorious view of the cleavage she now had. Despite her lissome figure, the dress had sort of squeezed everything together. Tony dragged his gaze up to meet April's. "The man's head looks like a balliard bill," he croaked, not even listening to himself. "How can he not know he's bald?"

"Pure, unadulterated denial." She shrugged; her cleavage deepened. "Anyway, my idea is that we can use Godfrey—and his muscles—to confront the thugs."

Although Tony's brain was working at a sluggish pace, he was still alert enough to realize that not all of April's story jibed. "I thought you hadn't seen the thugs since last weekend. How can we confront them when we don't know who or where they are?"

"You, being an investigator, can uncover their identities, of course." She straightened, her gaze sliding away from his. "And then there was that car following me during the scavenger hunt. It even parked outside your office building while I was inside. I didn't actually see who was driving it, but..."

Looking for a silly playboy named Donkey was one thing. Confronting thugs was another. Tony reluctantly acknowledged that he was out of his depth. But how could he confess that to April? She had such a touching faith in him, fraud that he was. Hell, she probably thought of him as a hero. The hard-boiled Sam Spade of her misbegotten dreams.

"That does it." Tony got to his feet, knowing there was no way of avoiding it. "We have to go to the police."

April's voice halted his march to the door. "No. We can't do that."

He turned back, quirking his eyebrows. "Why not?"

She laced her fingers together nervously and looked down at her boots. "Because Dunky stole my Fogbottom."

APRIL SLID A DISC of Annie-Lennox-sings-the-semirock-classics into the CD player, at the same time spinning the steering wheel with her left hand as she made a sharp turn off Lake Shore Drive. The car, an impractical foreign-made white convertible that had been her first purely frivolous purchase back in San Francisco, took the turn better than Tony. He slammed into the gearshift. She glanced down, saw that he hadn't injured anything vital, and broodingly regretted the extinction of bench seats.

Ah, well. *C'est la vie.*

"Let's recap," Tony said, looking worried as he raked one hand through his gleaming black hair. "Donkey asked you for money. A lot of money. When you turned him down, he stole something called a Fogbottom—"

"It's a painting. A very, very valuable painting."

"Okay, a painting. What I don't get is why you haven't reported the theft to the police."

"Well, they'd arrest Dunky, wouldn't they? I don't want to get him into trouble, especially when I'm sure he means to return it."

"He's probably fenced it by now, April."

It gave her a tiny thrill to hear Tony talk like that. So P.I. Still, she shook her head, biting her lip to stop herself from blurting out her suspicions of the real reason Dunky had appropriated the painting. "Donkey—uh, Dunky wouldn't do that."

"Your faith in a man named after an ass is truly touching."

"Sarcasm doesn't become you," April retorted with a blithe smile. Annie was winding up "Take Me to the River," which was pretty good timing, considering that they were heading for the ritzy lakeshore estate that sheltered the nest-of-vipers Dunkington clan. At the thought, April's smile slowly dissolved. The Dunkingtons' infighting made the Pierces' iceberg environment on Nob Hill look as friendly as Mr. Roger's Neighborhood. Almost.

"Why does Donkey need money?" asked Tony.

To stall, she pretended an absorption in humming along with "A Whiter Shade of Pale." By the time La Lennox got to the "sixteen vestal virgins," April was singing with gusto, half wishing she could go back to being one herself now that she'd found the gorgeous Tony Farentino. She just knew he'd be a better lover than her husband had been—maybe even good enough to wipe away the lingering self-doubt that was her legacy from Freeman Pierce. A bit shocked at herself for having such carnal thoughts so soon, she sang even louder.

"April," Tony admonished.

She finished the song on a lusty warble as they left Chicago behind, trying to decide if there was any reason to keep quiet about Dunky's gambling debts. Tony had to have *something* to work with. "Dunky has a teensy addiction to gambling," she finally admitted. Teensy as in one hundred and fifty thousand dollars' worth.

"I see." Tony's eyelids lowered to a lazy half-mast as he studied her. Pinpricks of effervescence danced across the surface of April's skin in response. She stroked her palm along the outside of her thigh, trying to smooth away the sensation.

His hot, coffee-colored eyes followed the motion. "The Dunkington family is rolling in dough," he continued in a strangled voice. "Wouldn't any of them help him out?"

"Hah! You haven't met MacArthur, Sugar and Talon yet. You'll find that all three are appropriately named." April had been introduced to Dunky not long after arriving in Chicago. While his funny, flamboyant, laissez-faire persona had distracted her from her recent troubles, the empathy they'd shared over similar family situations was what had really forged their strong friendship. At a time when she was still reeling with the effects of declaring her freedom from in-laws nearly as venal as the Dunkingtons, April had needed Dunky as much as he'd needed her. They'd cheered each other up, and on.

She usually tried not to think about those bleak days, those bad times. Being The Madcap Heiress was her refuge.

Tony was still mulling over the case. "Then we can assume the thugs are simply looking for Donkey to collect what he owes to his bookie."

"Or to break his legs, pull out his fingernails, drill his teeth and *then* collect." April frowned into the rearview mirror, then reached up to adjust the angle. "Poor Dunky," she said in a vague tone. She pulled off her sunglasses and stared into the side-view mirror, hoping it wasn't true that objects may be closer than they appear.

"He was probably smart to get out of town for a while." Tony stretched out, totally relaxed, tucking his arms behind his head.

What kind of a detective was he? her brain screamed. Did he have no observational skills whatsoever?

"Maybe you should let it slide, April. Stay away from the thugs altogether."

"Too late!" she shouted, and stomped on the accelerator. Horn blaring, the convertible shot through a busy intersection as the yellow light turned red. The black sedan that had been following them was stuck behind a station wagon.

"Hot damn," April crowed. "Am I good, or what?"

"My God." Tony twisted around and squinted into the wind. "Was it the thugs? Which car were they in?"

"Look behind the matron in the Volvo wagon. *Hoo-wheeeee*," she hooted triumphantly as they rocketed down the street.

The car careened around a corner. "Why would they be following you?" Tony shouted, leaning into the centrifugal force.

"Maybe they thought I'd lead them to Dunky." April spotted a fast-food joint on the left and screeched across three lanes of traffic to get to it. The car bumped over a curb and landed in the parking lot with a bone-rattling jounce.

Tony ricocheted off the dash. "Whath are you doing?" He hung his head over the door and spit blood onto the pavement. "I bith my thongue."

"Watch this," April said, pointing her chin at the street as the convertible fishtailed into the drive-through lane, albeit facing the wrong way. A few seconds later, the black sedan sped by. She whooped again and dug for her purse.

Tony slumped down in the seat and prodded tentatively at his tongue. "Forgeth the burgerth," he said when April shouted an order into the crackling microphone. "Leth geth outh of here."

She reversed up to the window, tossed a twenty at the teenager in it and passed a paper cup of ice chips to Tony. Soon they were taking the roundabout route to Windenhall, April munching from a cardboard envelope of supersize chili fries while Tony iced his tongue. He pulled it out of the cup, screwing up his face and crossing his eyes as he attempted to assess the damage.

"All better?" she cooed.

He narrowed his eyes at her and stirred the pink-tinged mound of ice with his thumb. He mumbled something unintelligible, took her firmly by the nape with his cold fingers and kissed her. Hard. The convertible swerved.

"Ouch," he said, jerking back, the salt and spice from her chili fries burning his injured tongue.

She patted his thigh. "Poor, poor P.I."

Being put on a par with "Poor Dunky" was the final indignity. With a groan Tony dropped his head back against the candy-apple red leather headrest. "I surrender. Do with me what you will."

He didn't open his eyes until their safe arrival at the Dunkingtons' tranquil estate approximately fifteen minutes later. Windenhall was a Tudor mansion set on ten acres of manicured lawns, sculpted topiary and towering chestnut trees. Veddy, veddy British proper. Veddy, veddy stultifying.

April parked on the cobbled drive, thinking that while her grandparents' house hadn't been quite as confining— particularly when her globe-trotting parents were in residence—she was familiar enough with rigid, stifling expectations. And certainly with homes that were actually little more than lovely, well-appointed cages, she mentally added, thinking now of the expensive condo she'd shared with Freeman Pierce.

But she'd escaped that life. And perhaps she could help Dunky find his way out, too.

First, she'd have to *find* him. April opened the car door and swung her legs out with a flourish. She stood and tugged on her boots. Her Azzadine Alaia minidress rode up to an even more dangerous level and she skinned it back down the inches of bare thighs revealed above her lace stockings, watching Tony's face from beneath her lashes. His eyes were as glazed as a doughnut. Good. Maybe he wouldn't notice anything she didn't want him to notice once they got up to Dunky's aerie on the third floor.

Homer, the cadaverous butler, opened the door. He was a refined, snobbish, dry-as-dust version of Godfrey, outfitted in black serge and a pleated shirt with a starched white collar. "Hi," April said, playing Miss Merry Sunshine. "Is Dunky home?"

"Master Darryl has not yet returned, Miss Pierce."

"How long's he been gone?" Tony interjected. April shot him a squinty-eyed glare. He was checking her facts, which was so insulting. Why couldn't he make this easier on both of them by just believing her semitrue story?

Homer's scraggly white eyebrows, the only hair on his head, lifted two inches, his lofty expression saying "Who are *you* and why should I deign to speak to you?"

"This is Tony Farentino," April introduced. "He's a...friend." No need to mention his profession yet. "Tony, Homer. He buttles." She didn't know if it was the done thing to introduce a visitor to the butler, but she'd come to despise snooty attitudes and would do as she pleased.

Apparently Homer didn't appreciate her egalitarianism. He sniffed, refusing to defrost. "I personally haven't seen Master Darryl since the family cocktail hour, Saturday evening. Miss Pierce, no doubt, can corroborate his later appearance elsewhere."

"No doubt," Tony said with some irony. April realized that he must be fully informed as far as the Picasso swing-set folly went, whereas the incident was a bit fuzzy in her own mind. Champagne cocktails at the Palmer House, if she remembered correctly.

"Is Mac—Arthur here?" she asked, doubting it because The General of Dunkington, Inc. would surely be off conglomerating, but wanting to be sure. When Homer said no, she asked for Sugar, Dunky's sweet as jelly, spineless as a jellyfish mother.

"Mrs. Dunkington is at a charity function." Unlike her dear Godfrey's characteristic rumble, Homer's voice purred as smoothly as a Rolls-Royce.

"Is it okay if we go up to Dunky's suite anyway? To check things out?" April made her lower lip tremble. "I'm awfully worried about him." Tony watched in wordless admiration.

Homer hesitated, then said crisply, "I think not." April sighed and slumped her shoulders with a hangdog sadness. Homer put on the stiff upper lip. "It would not be proper, Miss Pierce."

She straightened with a jaunty toss of her head. "Okay, Homer." Walking away, she waved as the butler closed the door. "See you around."

Tony stared after her. "I thought you could get us in."

"I can. Just give me two seconds." She came back up the stone steps and pressed her ear to the door. "Just as I thought. It's teatime at the old homestead. They'll all be in the kitchen. Now, shh, follow me." Despite its creaky antique appearance and hammered brass hinges, the door opened without a sound. The vast entry hall was dark and silent, the paneled walls lined with gloomy portraits of pompous donkey-behind Dunkingtons. April took Tony's hand and scurried up the massive half-timber staircase toward the somber reaches of the second and third floors.

Dunky's home-inside-a-house was a suite of leather, walnut and paisley-patterned rooms that appeared to have been furnished by Ralph Lauren during his Englishmen's-club phase. "What are we looking for?" Tony whispered, tiptoeing past a maroon leather armchair and a butler's table chockablock with cut-glass decanters and liquor bottles.

"You're the P.I." April went into the bedroom, lifted the hunter green duvet and knelt to peer under the sleigh bed. "You tell me."

"The Fogbottom?" he suggested.

"Mmm. Or a flight schedule to Bora Bora."

Tony picked a photographic slide off the floor and held it up to the murky light filtering past the heavy window dressings. "Maybe even a Maltese Falcon. You wouldn't be putting me on, would you, Ap—"

"Shhh," she said. "I hear footsteps."

"Then you must have the ears of a—"

"Someone's coming!" April whisked Tony past a cubbyhole filled with art supplies and into a ten-by-twelve cedar closet that was as well stocked as Marshall Field's men's department.

"Wait," he said. "We should check out the studio. Who knows? Your stolen painting could be sitting out in plain sight." There'd been stacks of canvases, apparently mostly nudes at a glimpse. Maybe one of the bare bottoms was a Fogbottom.

"Oh, hush, will you?" April whispered. "I don't care about the Fogbottom, I care about Dunky." That much, as far as it went, was strictly the truth. One thing she was sure of was that people were more important than possessions. And, furthermore, that people were not meant to *be* possessions.

She shoved Tony toward a cubicle stuffed with cashmere robes and silk dressing gowns, then eased the door open an inch. A faint whirring sound came from the sitting room. "It must be Harriet, the maid. She's vacuuming."

Tony's voice was muffled by Dunky's loungewear. "Since we're stuck here for the duration, why don't you tell me about the Fogbottom?" He pushed aside an embroidered Chinese robe, looped his arm around April's waist and pulled her into the cubicle. His hand drifted down to the curves of her shrink-wrapped bottom. "What does it depict? A full moon shrouded by a pea soup fog?"

"You think you're so funny." April squirmed against his chest, trying to keep her face straight despite her

roused sense of humor and her fizzing nerve endings.
"Lesley Orville Fogbottom was a preeminent British artist of the mid 1800s. It just so happens that he specialized
in nudes."

"And, by a great coincidence, so does Donkey."

Yikes. If Tony had already noticed that, he might soon
figure out what Dunky intended to do with the "borrowed" Fogbottom. Then Dunky would be in even more
trouble than he was now...

Biting her lip, April scanned Tony's face from beneath
her lowered eyelashes. Obviously his eyes hadn't been as
glazed as she'd hoped. In fact, he looked less like a pastry than any man she'd ever met—although he certainly
qualified as mouth-watering.

He did have that marvelously deep tan and those stunning angular cheekbones. He also had adorable shallow
dimples in his cheek and his chin. And espresso eyes with
long lashes and laugh lines etched at the corners, and hair
as blue-black as midnight. He was perhaps a few inches
too tall for her, but—she braced her hands against his
hard, muscular chest and gazed up into his eyes—they
probably could work something out. Or at least have lots
of fun trying.

"Do private eyes spend a lot of time stuck in closets?"
she whispered. Judging by his tan, definitely not. She
wondered if he'd recently been on vacation. Chicago had
been having a very rainy spring.

"Only when they're dumb enough to accept madcap
heiresses as clients," Tony whispered in return.

"Don't give me that. You're loving it."

He grinned and squeezed her a little tighter. "Okay, I
have to admit..."

Mischief shone in April's eyes. "How's the tongue?"

"Still working."

"But are you absolutely sure it's fully functioning?"
She licked her lips. "No more salt."

The whirring vacuum had moved into the bedroom. If they were going to be caught they might as well be caught doing something really good. She nestled against him, tilted her head back—and registered the empty hook behind Tony's head just before he leaned down and blocked it out.

His lips descended on hers, firm and warm and darkly sweet. The brief, hard kiss in the car had been a throwaway gesture, but this one really meant something.

He kisses with such emotion, April thought with startled pleasure, stiffening for a split second at the unaccustomed revelation before reflexively softening into a slump. Tony held her tight to his chest, taking her along as he tilted back into the clinging depths of Dunky's closet. She smiled against his mouth, parting her lips and sinking into the dual embrace of strong male arms and the luxurious, enfolding fabrics. Very appropriate. The inside of Tony's lips felt like wet silk, his tongue—fully functioning, oh, my, yes!—like velvet. His hands slid down her body in a long caress, making her weak, making her swoon, making her tremble with appreciation at his prowess.

She recognized the scintillating sensations he produced in her even though they were unfamiliar. Hadn't she longed for this in her most private fantasies?

His tongue lashed hers gently as it probed, deepening the kiss, then withdrew, then returned. Tony, seemingly so stolid and by-the-book, was a bit of a tease. It was an intoxicating discovery, and April murmured her delight.

The heaviness in her heart slowly began to dissipate as the kiss continued. Although Freeman had branded her the Snow Queen, perhaps she'd been more of a Sleeping Beauty all along, simply waiting for the appropriate hero to wake her up. Her husband had turned out to be a villain in disguise, and none of the Palace Circle Prankster playboys had seemed likely. Only Tony, darling, darling

Tony, had managed to awaken her libido with one incredible kiss!

"What a prince," she said dazedly once he'd finally dragged his mouth from hers.

Tony shook his head, looking somewhat confounded himself. With a visible effort, he regrouped to scold her with a terse *"Shhh."*

She giggled imprudently. "Kissing me again would be a surefire way to keep me quiet—"

Instead he clamped his palm over her mouth. "Listen. That kiss might've been good—okay, *great*—but it was still a mistake." His hushed voice revealed regret as he whispered into her ear, his lips not quite touching but tickling deliciously. "You're my client," he insisted. "Sort of."

April's vociferous protest didn't make it past his hand, so she wriggled against him, trying to wrench herself away. The heel of her boot accidentally came down on Tony's instep and he fell sideways with a grunt of pain. Flailing at Dunky's nightwear as she lost her own balance, April collapsed atop him with a yelp.

"Oops," she puffed, crawling backward off him on her hands and knees. "Sorry." She stopped to strip a scarlet silk pajama top from her head.

"Not as sorry as you're going to be if the maid catches us," Tony hissed. "Ouch." He pulled a hard satin slipper with an Arabic *Thousand and One Nights* upturned toe out from beneath him and tossed it into the opposite corner. The slipper thudded to the carpet with a jingle of the bell dangling at its curled tip.

The vacuum switched off. April and Tony froze. There came a too-close-for-comfort clatter of an easel from the cubbyhole studio. They turned in unison toward the sound. Sudden panic made April forget her reasons why Tony should keep kissing her and remember something Dunky had told her about his teenage adventures when

General MacArthur, otherwise known as dear old Dad, Arthur Dunkington, had confined him to quarters. At the time, the story had no more importance than bringing to mind her own childhood retreats into the fantasyland of movies and fairy tales. Now it promised an escape hatch.

She crawled over and whispered into Tony's ear. "Let's get out of here."

"Window?" he mouthed with skepticism. He leaned as far away from her as he could get and unwound the pajama bottoms from his neck.

April hoisted herself up and went over to slide the window open. Without hesitation, she clambered through it as easily as if she were rolling out of bed, then turned to urge Tony to follow. He did, moving methodically, remembering to shut the window behind him. Finding themselves on a narrow ledge, they skidded on their backsides down the angled roof to a flat section fifteen feet below and edged along it until they came to the wide expanse of slate and glass that roofed a first-floor sunroom. April paused to take a deep breath, blinking at the suddenness of their expulsion from sensuous darkness to sunny daylight.

"Dunky told me he used to climb down the trellis when he had to sneak out," she explained, neglecting to mention that her friend had done it at age fifteen, before his One Great Love, identified by anyone else as éclairs, had become quite so evident around his midriff.

Tony pressed his palms to the sun-warmed slate. "You're going to scratch your thighs on this."

"I'll keep my legs up," she said, but he removed his black vest and wrapped it around her exposed skin. Trying to hold it in place made for awkward maneuvering as they inched down the steep roof, but April was too touched by the gallantry of the gesture to complain. "Speaking of men's garments," she said once they'd successfully reached the eaves and she got her voice back.

"Dunky took his favorite quilted satin smoking jacket with him. I saw the empty hook back in the closet."

"So?" Tony lay on his stomach, reached over the gutter and shook the trellis. The dark green leaves of the clematis clinging to it shivered. A few pink petals drifted to the velvety lawn.

April sat in a cross-legged slant and admired the exquisite athleticism of Tony's sprawled form. She'd certainly hired the right man; he was so admirably competent. The muscles in his shoulders shifted beneath the taut chambray of his shirt as he levered himself up and looked back at her. "So that means he planned his disappearance," she panted, still short of breath, but not entirely because of their perilous descent.

"Maybe he spilled port on it and it's being laundered."

"Oh, Tony, you're so pragmatic." She reverted to her Kate-Hepburn-as-the-madcap-heiress accent. "*Such* a bore."

"The obvious is usually obvious for a reason."

April shoved him affectionately even though her hands wanted to linger. "Get out of here."

"As you wish." He swung his long legs over the side. "If I break any bones will you nurse me back to health, Lola?"

She angled down to kiss him lightly. "Yes." For a moment she held his face between her palms. "Are you having fun yet?"

"Scads, Miss Pierce," he said, putting on his own accent. It sounded like a garbled Godfrey/Homer/Cary Grant hybrid. With the emphasis, unfortunately, on the garble. "Absolute scads."

She hung her head over the edge and watched him climb down, then took to the trellis herself after buttoning the vest around her hips so it at least partly concealed her bottom half. Although her prince of a private eye had certainly performed above and beyond the call of duty so far, he didn't deserve *that* big a reward.

April threw back her head and laughed gaily, then nimbly scrambled down the trellis into Tony's waiting arms.

_3_

Half Woman, Half Talon

TONY SPENT THE REMAINDER OF THE DAY reading back
issues of newspapers at the library to avoid Miss Estelle's
silent but deadly glares because running the gamut of
butlers had swept the appointment at Em-Tee Tech out of
his mind. He arrived at the town house that evening
knowing more, yet still curiously little, about April Pierce.

He'd discovered that she'd swept into Chicago seemingly out of the blue six months ago. There were refer-
ences to the wealth and upper-crustness of the San
Francisco Pierces, but no actual firm connection was es-
tablished between them and April. The lady in question,
temporarily installed in a deluxe suite at a ritzy hotel that
catered to her every whim, chose to maintain her air of
mystery. Chicago society had welcomed her with open
arms. Within weeks she'd bought a house and officially
become The Madcap Heiress, the leader of the flamboyant younger set.

Their various shenanigans had been well documented
in the cloying style of gossip columnists. One had gleefully coined the name "Palace Circle Pranksters," which
had stuck. By midafternoon, Tony had followed April
and her band of merrymakers from a twelve-course tail-
gate party at Soldier Field where April had been photo-
graphed eating a bratwurst atop a Mercedes, swaddled
head to toe in a kicky hot pink fake fur, to an incident at

the Lincoln Park Zoo where the Pranksters had unsuccessfully attempted to liberate a baby leopard.

It was all too much—too much of the same. Tony had left the library with no more insight into the true April Pierce than what he'd gleaned yesterday. Namely, that she had an extremely keen sense of hearing but sang off-key, that she relished absurdity and pooh-poohed stuffiness despite her *beaucoup* bucks, was quite daring when it came to breaking and entering and getaway driving, and liked to color-coordinate her ensembles right down to the hue of her cute little electric blue underpants.

So who was April Pierce? He wasn't sure.

But he was definitely going to find out. He'd just have to refrain from kissing her as he had.

Good luck.

Tony twirled the bell, pressed his ear to a leering satyr and didn't hear a sound until Godfrey yanked open the door. Caught eavesdropping, he tried to look innocent. "Why, hello, there, Godfrey, my good man. I'm here to pick up April. Is she ready?"

Godfrey scowled, apparently not recognizing Tony's Cary. "Salon," he grunted, and clumped through the pink marble foyer to a door at the far end, his bulk wrapped in an XXX-Large white chef's apron.

"Come in, Tony," April called from the salon. "Don't mind Godfrey. He's upset because I'm missing dessert. He does make a fabulous lemon-raspberry soufflé."

"I figured there had to be some reason besides his impeccable manner that you keep him around." Already knowing to expect another of April's incarnations, Tony entered the jewel-box salon with anticipation. And stopped dead. "My God. You're beautiful."

April curtsied. "Thank you, darling Tony."

This is awful, he thought. *How am I going to resist her?*

She stood in the glow of the refracted, sparkling lights of the chandelier, wearing a long, slim column of golden silk charmeuse. The bodice was draped in deep V's front and back, and even under her arms, so that Tony was agonized by a display of lots of fair skin and terrible, tantalizing glimpses of the inner and outer curves of her breasts. What was worse, the entire garment was held up only by thin topaz-beaded straps, the kind that a man with little self-control might bite through just to see the dress puddle at her feet.

Awful. Horrendous. Hell on earth. And he could just imagine the tiny triangle of gold silk that was no doubt glimmering across her sassy derriere at this very moment!

"Anything wrong?" she asked with a tinkling laugh.

"You look..." He swallowed the lump in his throat. "You look like a trophy. Like the little person on top of a trophy. All gold, I mean."

"Is that good?"

"On you, yes," he said, blinking. She was a veritable haze of gold, from the nimbus of her golden hair to the metallic sandals on her feet. His gaze slowly traveled up the gleaming dress to her face. Her eyes were gold, too. An exotic, enchanting, very unlikely shade of gold.

He stared. "Didn't your eyes used to be blue?"

"Contacts, Tony. I have an entire wardrobe of them. Seventeen pairs. Five shades of blue, four green, one each of silver, gold, lavender and violet, and four browns, from chocolate to amber." She batted her lashes. "I live to accessorize."

Tony slowly shook his head. He was thunderstruck. Dazed. Agog. He'd wanted to get to know the real April Pierce, and here she wasn't, still as elusive as a dream, as insubstantial as a ghost. He wondered if there was anything about her that was genuine. And he wondered again if she could be manipulating him. He was supposed to detest that, but at the moment he was having trouble remembering why. "So what's the natural color of your eyes?'' he asked, working up his suspicions as he reminded himself that ghosts haunted and dreams contained hidden meanings.

"Maybe I'll tell you one day...when we know each other better. A girl can't give away all her secrets on the first date." She smiled prettily and picked up a fringed shawl, a filmy triangle threaded with gold. "Shall we go?"

Tony had no choice but to shrug off his uneasiness and offer her his arm. They'd made plans to attend an opening at Talon Dunkington's art gallery. April was sure that meeting Dunky's friends and the rest of the players would put Tony into the game and perhaps provide his keen investigatory instincts with the clue that would lead them to Dunky.

Yeah, right.

GALERIE DIABOLIQUE specialized in surreal art of the fantastical, sensual, soulless sort. Tonight, gigantic paintings of luridly posed half-animal alien women dominated the lucent white walls of Talon's converted redbrick warehouse on Superior Street.

"That one looks like you," Tony said, following April as she confidently plunged into the Friday-night crowd. At least a dozen of the guests waved and squealed greetings at her.

April looked at a spooky moonscape of a birdwoman crouched beside a pile of bleached bones. Gemstones and silver blade points had been glued to the canvas as eyes, teeth and claws. Wings the same lime green as her peacock costume were folded beside the creature's satiny bare breasts. Despite the feathers, her expression was feline.

"Gosh." April's gold eyes widened. Although she liked testing out other identities, she wasn't sure this was one she'd choose. "Thanks...I think."

Tony put his mouth near her ear so she could hear him above the voluble crowd. "There's something very sensual about her. She's a huntress."

A regal Indian woman in a sari brushed past April, forcing her to press back into Tony. The silk of her dress was so thin she could feel his thighs warm and hard against her bottom. A shivery fizz of awareness swept through her, a sensation not unlike the tiny bubbles bursting in the glasses of champagne held by many of the guests. April adored champagne; this was the first time she'd met a man who could reproduce its effect on her body a hundredfold, apparently without even trying.

What would happen, she wondered, when Tony really made an effort? Her pulse shuddered with anticipation. And, perhaps, with a touch of wariness. Since their first kiss, she'd come back to her senses enough to realize that their mutual attraction could well be too powerful to maintain at a purely frivolous level. While she wasn't averse to living the fairy tale, she'd learned not to believe in the "happily ever after" part. Tony was the kind of guy to demand more of her than she was prepared to give— and she wasn't thinking only of sex. Love was what she truly feared.

April turned cautiously, inching her body away from the heat of his. "She looks like she could tear her quarry from limb to limb with those teeth. I've never been that voracious."

"Voracious? Hmm . . . maybe you haven't known the right men."

The timbre of his voice was low and sexy, but April stiffened as the words prompted a fleeting mental image of her unhappy conjugal bed. "Weren't we talking about quarries?" she quipped, forcing the defiant lightheartedness she'd adopted to keep such thoughts at bay. She nudged Tony in the ribs. "Or is it the same thing?"

"I'll be your quarry if you'll be my huntress—uh-oh, on second thought, you don't look like the woman in the painting at all. *She* does. And I don't mean that as a compliment." Tony indicated a woman in off-the-shoulder bloodred satin who was slinking through the crowd with the sinuous grace of a panther, scarcely pausing to brush aside the less important patrons who were trying to get her attention. "That's Talon Dunkington, or I miss my guess."

"Bingo," April whispered in his ear as Talon arrived.

"So glad you could make it, April, dear. A Dante Vincennes painting would look marvelous in your town house, don't you agree?" Talon leaned in for an air-kiss, her cool ebony gaze sliding to Tony. Her eyes narrowed. She lifted one elegant hand and touched a bloodred talon to her bloodred lips. "And who is this? Your latest devotee?"

"This is Tony Farentino. He's a private investigator." April put her hand behind her back and found Tony's. Their fingers intertwined. "I've hired him to look for your brother."

Talon's laugh was sharper than the blade points in the painting. "You're not still harping on Dunky's so-called disappearance! I'm sure he's simply enjoying a few days at the gaming tables in Monaco." When she caught Tony's interested eye, she modulated her voice. "It's not the first time our dear Dunky has made himself scarce at an opportune moment."

"Hasn't he run out of funds?" April asked.

Talon shrugged negligently, her shoulders very white against a ruby necklace and the shining wings of her precision-cut black bob. "That's what charge cards are for, sweet April."

Tony studied Talon. A darkly handsome but chilly woman, she seemed the antithesis of April's blond charm and insouciance. Although Talon was careful to appear nonchalant, her eyes betrayed an incisive interest in Dunky's location. He couldn't tell for sure whether or not she knew anything about her brother's disappearance, but he'd guess yes. "I take it you haven't heard from him?" he probed.

Her bee-stung, silicone lips smiled. "I didn't expect to."

"Well, I think there's something wrong," April said stoutly. "I *know* there's something wrong." Tony squeezed her hand.

Talon, scanning the crowd, said nothing.

"We have to find him before the thu—" April began, but Talon interrupted her with a tarted-up sales spiel promoting the artist of the evening. Detecting a hint of desperation in the pitch, Tony wondered about the state of her finances. Then again, tonight's attendance was certainly impressive, and by the looks of it, the guests were well-heeled.

When April expressed no inclination toward writing out a check, Talon spotted a likelier prospect and abruptly excused herself. She was blowing kisses to her next victim before they'd even said goodbye.

Tony watched as she joined a small man with a goatee, a raw silk designer suit and an acquisitive air. "Who's that?" he asked April out of idle curiosity.

"Nelson McNair," she answered, equally idly. "A big deal collector, I hear. A few months ago, Talon was after me to sell the Fogbottom to her so she could resell it to McNair. At a huge markup, I'm sure."

Now that was interesting. "So Talon doesn't restrict herself to selling these kinds of modern technotronic things?" he asked, eyeballing a painting with the square footage of a small room. Just a little something to hang above the sofa. It depicted a robotic shemale astride a leopardlike horned beast. Blood dripped from both their fangs.

"Um, I thought she did. But I guess not."

"Is Talon simply greedy, or are both the Dunkington siblings wanting for ready cash?"

April cocked her head thoughtfully. "As far as I know, she's just greedy."

"One can never have too much money, right?"

"One certainly can," April said blackly, taking two flutes of champagne from a passing waiter. Tony declined, so she drank hers then his in a few gulps.

"Is Talon greedy enough to deal in stolen goods?"

April gasped. "Tony! You don't think . . . ?"

"Why not? Donkey could have sold her the Fogbottom out of desperation."

"He did not. I know he didn't because—" April snapped her mouth shut.

"Because?"

"Because . . ." she repeated. "Because then he'd have paid off his bookie! The thugs wouldn't've had a reason to follow us yesterday."

"I suppose that's true," Tony said slowly, but April didn't like the speculative gleam in his eye.

He was altogether too keen, especially considering that this was a case that she preferred not to see *completely* solved. While she wanted to discover Dunky's whereabouts, and hopefully recover her painting in the process, she didn't want to be the person responsible for sending her misguided friend to the State of Illinois Big House.

A distraction for Tony was what she needed. April looked around the crowded gallery, picking out familiar faces and waving them over. There was no one better at creating a diversion than the Palace Circle Pranksters. For the past several months they'd been just the tonic whenever she'd needed an antidote for the doldrums.

Ten minutes later, Tony was at the center of a glittering, gabbling group of hoity-toities in formal dress. They had first names like Sistie, Gunther, Ju-Ju, Desmond . . . and last names that gave off a definite odor of greenbacks. They laughed a lot, talked a lot, smoked and drank a lot. April spun among them dizzily, a flighty golden princess with flushed cheeks and a determinedly jaunty smile. It seemed to Tony that she was trying too hard. He listened warily as the Pranksters planned to lay siege to a club called Monkeyshines and dance till dawn. They urged him to join them.

He didn't want to be one of the gang. Their money didn't impress him, nor their triviality. He'd rather April saw him as an individual, a unique, worthy, honorable, valued individual. Which might be quite a feat, considering that he had essentially lied about who he was.

Get off it, buddy, said the moody part of him that was still wallowing in despair and cynicism. A woman with April's money and prestige probably thought of a man like himself as no more than a momentarily amusing accessory. Her very own P.I.

He'd already wrangled with these people—the type who could buy and sell lesser mortals and were perfectly willing to do so—during his tenure hearing. And lost miserably because he'd thought scholarly work still outweighed possessing the right pedigree.

Tony knew it would be sensible to listen to the skeptical inner voice that asked him why he should tell her the truth, why he should care what she thought. But it was tough to keep up such a mood around a woman like April Pierce, even when her merriment was forced.

Impulsively he caught her arm as she flitted past him. He had to tell her the truth about his occupation and he had to do it tonight.

"We have to talk," he said.

She leaned in. "About the case? Oh, I think we've done enough investigating for one night." She playfully tugged the lapel of his rented tux. "You can fraternize with a client just this once, can't you? Have some fun, fun, fun?"

"April, baby!" interjected a suave male-model type. His features were so chiseled they'd have made Rodin proud. "If it's midnight, it must be time to tango!" he cried, holding out his arms and swiveling his hips to an imaginary Latin beat.

Although April giggled appreciatively, she tucked herself beneath Tony's circling arm. "I think Tony and I will be skipping the dancing tonight."

"Party pooper," Mr. Tango said, but his disappointment was fleeting. He grabbed the next gorgeous woman who caught his eye and repeated the line to her. More receptive than April, she danced off through the crowd with him.

"Are you sure you don't want to join your friends?" Tony asked dutifully, even as he maneuvered April out of the circle of Pranksters and toward a steel staircase that wound up to the second level, where the throng thronged less thickly.

She trotted up the steps, glancing sidelong at him, flashing a flirty smile. "I have my priorities straight."

Thinking she was referring to him, and maybe to a higher set of standards, Tony's spirits lifted. Then he realized she probably meant their search for Donkey. The gnawing sensation in his gut carried the slight tang of jealousy. Perhaps it was time he found out more about her relationship with Darryl Dunkington, who was by all accounts a notorious do-nothing playboy. Knowing for sure that April went for that kind of guy would definitely hammer home the realization that she and Tony had no future. Despite her allure, it would simply be impossible.

Impossible? He wondered. Was anything truly impossible?

Okay, maybe it was just extremely unlikely.

"April, where are you going?" called a woman in black lace and platinum hair extensions. "We're about to leave for the club."

April leaned over the long coiled sheet of brushed steel that was the stair rail. "Go on without me. Maybe Tony and I will catch up later."

"Not in this lifetime," he muttered as they reached the second floor.

"Sistie will be so disappointed," April said glibly. "You made quite an impression on her. I believe I even heard the phrase 'Greek god' mentioned."

He smiled. "Now which one was she?"

"None of your business!" She laughed as he guided her past more woman-beast portraiture to the back of the second level, where she'd told him there was a private office. They ducked into a small room done completely in shades of white to show off the stoplight triptych of large, round, red, green and amber canvases on one wall.

April sat on the corner of the ivory Parsons desk and crossed her arms. "So what's this about?" Her tone was edgy. "You're being very autocratic, darling Tony. I'm not sure I care for that."

Now that he had her undivided attention, Tony didn't know how to present the truth about his deception. He cleared his throat. *April, I've been meaning to tell you…?* No, that sounded totally weak. Coughing, he tugged at the tight collar of his formal white shirt. He felt a lot more comfortable in sweat-soaked khaki. "See, the thing is…" He took a deep breath. "I'm not a private detective. I'm an archaeologist."

She rolled her eyes in exaggerated disbelief. "And I'm really a peacock!" Chuckling in amusement, she carelessly leaned back on her arms and bumped a sleek vanilla-colored telephone. Glancing down, she noticed that a red light was lit on the base. Thinking she'd accidentally pressed one of the buttons, she poked one at random to see if the light would turn off. A click and a burring noise was broadcast over the telephone's intercom system.

"But it's true," Tony was saying as he took a laminated college ID card out of his wallet. "I also teach—used to teach—at . . ."

April wasn't paying attention. She pressed the button again, successfully shutting off the intercom, then tried another. She picked up the receiver to listen for the dial tone. A female voice spoke into her ear. ". . . asking questions. I need Dunky to deliver that painting soon."

April clapped her hand over her mouth as she slid limply off the desk. Frantically she waved Tony over to listen in.

She held the telephone up between them. He put his hand over the mouthpiece. ". . . an eager buyer with a quarter of a million dollars and a hugely inflated sense of his own expertise," Talon was saying. Tony looked at April with an I-told-you-so expression.

"Yeah, sure, *Miz* Dunkton," replied an uncouth male voice. "Problem is your little brother ain't showing his face at none of the tracks. I even sent T-Bone up to Wisconsin to check out the dog races."

"Keep looking," Talon said with obvious distaste. "He'll turn up."

A heavy sigh. "Then we gotta have more for expenses."

"You'll be paid," Talon snapped. "Money's not our present problem. April Pierce and her private investigator are." Tony felt April tense. He pried the phone out of her hands.

"I'll be glad to take care of them, especially *her,*" the unidentified male said with a menacing leer, and April gasped a startled *"Oh!"* of shock.

"What was that?" Talon screeched. "Is there someone on this line? Jody? Jody, is that you? I'm going to kill—" Her rage was cut off midhowl when she disconnected the line.

"This is just great." Quietly Tony replaced the telephone. "Where is Talon's office?"

"I think it's on the third floor," April said with a shrug. She didn't seem to realize their situation, just stabbed her fists onto her hips and glared at the phone. "Can you believe that? Talon is nothing but a two-bit—"

"Later," interrupted Tony. He cracked the office door, peeked out, then shut it and grabbed April's hand. "I'm having a bad case of déjà vu. Let's hope we don't have to take to the rooftops again." He pulled her to the only other door in the room, a slider of brushed steel.

April picked up her skirt and followed him into a narrow storage closet lined with racks of shrouded artwork. He'd just closed the door when Talon burst into the office. "Jody?" she demanded. "Jody, are you in here?" A thin line of light appeared beneath the door. Swearing under her breath, Talon grabbed the telephone, punched several buttons and slammed it back down.

April crouched in the spare inches of space between one of the racks and the wall. Tony edged into a dark corner behind a seven-foot celestial being made of papier-mâché and copper wire. A moment later, the door slid open.

Fortunately Talon's inspection was brief. She flicked on the light—Tony and April exchanged wide-eyed stares— but then she took only one step into the closet. After a moment of silence, she hissed another oath, hit the light switch and retreated. When the office door slammed Tony decided it was safe to breathe again.

"Wow, that was thrilling." April's voice sparkled with vivacity as she wiggled out from behind the rack. "An honest-to-goodness, cloak-and-dagger close call!"

Earlier, Tony had thought her enjoyment seemed forced this evening, but her reaction now was genuine. "I can't believe it," he said as he left his corner. "We get stuck in another closet and you're having fun."

She put her arms around his waist and hugged him tight. Having grown up in a demonstrative family, he was used to touchy-feely types. But getting squeezed by April Pierce beat getting squeezed by his ouzo-breathed Grandpa Anapoulis any day.

Without letting go, she looked up at his face, her small chin resting on his chest. "That had to be one of the thugs Talon was talking to, don't you think?" She wriggled with delight. "Just imagine—we've uncovered a scam!"

If she wiggled that way once more, she wouldn't need imagination—she'd know exactly how he felt about her. He believed *blatantly obvious* was the correct phrase to use in such a situation. "We don't know yet what we've uncovered," he said, trying to concentrate on the case. "Remember, you first thought it was the bookie who hired the thugs, and that they were following you in hopes that you'd lead them to Donkey."

April cocked her head. "Well, that last part was right, but I guess Talon's the mastermind instead of the bookie."

"And she's willing to send the thugs after her own brother?"

"You bet. As long as he's got the Fogbottom."

"Which she intends to sell to McNair, even though it's stolen."

"Something like that."

Tony narrowed his eyes. April seemed awfully cavalier about the loss of her expensive painting. "Isn't this fun?" she said quickly, distracting him from his suspicions with another impulsive shimmy against the length of him. "I'm *sooo* excited!"

She had that right. Dumb but dangerous thugs and self-admonishments about keeping his and April's involvement at a businesslike level were no match for the physical reality of their instantaneous chemistry.

"Slow down, April," he said, trying to sound cautious even though there was excitement in his own voice. Excavating a career-making archaeological discovery amidst potentially devastating earthquake tremors had been perilous but exhilarating; larking around with April was downright stimulating. His pulse drummed with the rapid beat of a heavy-metal rocker.

Despite his earlier skepticism, he couldn't stop himself. He slid his hands up from her waist, over the tempting V's of bare skin at her sides, bracketed her arms and lifted her onto her toes so he could kiss her without bending his knees.

April's sigh was voluptuous with longing as she twined her arms around his shoulders. "Kiss me, Tony," she demanded, reveling in the dramatic command.

Danger ebbed as desire welled between them, so tangible Tony felt the air was thick with it. "You needn't have asked," he murmured, finding her lips as sweetly eager as he remembered. Kissing April was like drinking a cup of honeyed sunshine. His tongue probed deeply, gently, then, gradually, as hunger burgeoned, with more urgency.

She responded beautifully, pressing her body up into his, clinging along the length of him with her fingers laced at his nape. He skimmed his hands down her delicate rib cage, then back up to the soft outer curves of her breasts. He'd wanted to slip his hand under the gold silk of her gown all evening and not even the precariousness of their illicit location could stop him now.

"Don't—stop," April whispered, her voice catching as he put his hand over her bare breast and squeezed. "Oh, Tony, don't ever stop."

He rubbed his thumb across her puckered nipple. She gasped and sank to her heels, then immediately pushed herself back up on tiptoe, arching her back to return her breast to his palm. "That feels so good," she said, delighting him with a flurry of kisses.

"Yes." Although his eyes had gone dark with need, he made himself pull back—a few inches. He traced her parted lips with his fingertip. Knowing he shouldn't, he relented with a moan and kissed her again, then buried his face in the scented cloud of her hair. "Do you like this?" he whispered, touching the point of his tongue to the shell-like swirls of her ear, kissing her lobe and making her shiver.

"*Yesss.*" Her sibilant sigh of pleasure was abruptly cut off. "Hey, don't stop now," she protested as he did just that.

Slowly regaining some small amount of restraint, he'd begun to remember his doubts. And his intentions. Theirs was a professional relationship, more or less, making kissing, even fantastic kissing, inappropriate. But it was hard to force the words out. "April, this is neither the time nor the place." She didn't looked pleased, so he added lightly, "If we're caught, it'd be a straight drop to the street from *this* closet."

Her eyelids lowered. "Okay, so then when?" Her voice quavered—just a little. "Where?"

Tony realized that his hand was still inside her dress. Her breast was a small plump weight in his palm, the hardened peak poking out between his fingers. Reluctantly he withdrew. "I . . . don't know," he said haltingly. A lame answer, but the truth. At the moment, he didn't know anything except that his hand felt strangely empty and his body achingly deprived.

April dropped to her heels and rearranged the neckline of her dress. "I'm too impulsive for you." She bit her lower lip. "Too flamboyant." Then she smiled tentatively and added in a small voice, "Or maybe you're just not into closets?"

"Of course it's not you. It's me." Perhaps it was easier all around to blame his withdrawal on their business relationship. How convenient that he'd screwed that up, too. "I'm not who you think I am and I can't go on pretending—"

Except that, despite the conviction of his words, their next move had suddenly popped into his head. He had no idea where it came from, especially when he was on the verge of trying to convince April he really was an archaeologist, but it was too good to ignore. And its opportune timing would get him out of this difficult situation.

"Talon's office," he said. "Do you think we can sneak up there?"

April blinked in the darkness, startled by the abrupt change in subject. "Uh, I don't see why not." She rapidly recovered her daring. "Yes, sure, I'm game. But why?"

"Redial," Tony said succinctly. "Assuming it was Talon who placed the call, we can press the redial button on her telephone to find out the thug's location."

"Tony, that's brilliant." April rose on the balls of her feet to reward him with a quick kiss, then practically skipped to the door. "I can be the lookout while you sneak into her office."

She slid the door open and turned back to him, scolding him with a shake of her head. "And to think you were trying to tell me you're not a private investigator. Hah, a likely story!"

Even in the dim light, her eyes glowed a clear amber. The same color as a caution light, Tony reminded himself. While a woman as privileged as April Pierce could well afford to fling caution to the wind, he'd been practicing for years the methodical, painstaking methods of an archaeologist. Not even the admittedly potent influence of The Madcap Heiress could overcome such training... at least not so quickly. He must proceed cautiously—in all things.

Caution, he repeated to himself; the word blinking off and on in his mind's eye. *Caution,* caution, *caution.*

4

In the Palm of Her Hand

TALON'S VAST third-floor office was vacant. While April hovered near the balcony of the open reception area, goggling over the balustrade at the swirling kaleidoscope of color formed by the crowd forty-five feet below, Tony slipped inside the darkened office and located the telephone atop a sculptural steel-and-etched-glass desk.

April joined him as he picked up the receiver and pressed the redial button. Conveniently the number appeared simultaneously on a tiny screen with a luminous LCD readout. She snatched up a silver fountain pen and, after a futile search for scrap paper—the desk had no drawers, the wastebasket no waste—inked the sequence across her palm for safekeeping.

"What's your location?" Tony said in response to a muffled salutation on the other end of the line. April tried to listen in but he waved her away and toward the open door, making sawing motions across his throat with Talon's onyx-handled letter opener. April got the point.

Returning to the balcony, she identified a figure in ruby satin almost immediately. She pulled back in alarm when Talon's face turned up toward the loft, her lips a slash of red, her eyes like burn marks against her pale skin. April stood very still, a small shock rippling through her. *How far would Talon go to secure the Fogbottom? Was she not just greedy, but amoral, too?*

No longer quite so thrilled by her flirt with danger, April hurried past a knot of guests, her dress shimmering like molten gold. She had to retrieve Tony in case Talon had spotted April's surveillance and was on her way upstairs.

DESCENDING THE STAIRCASE, they met only a wraith of a girl in a baggy print dress and clunky buckled shoes. A limp reddish braid looped across her thin shoulder. Nestled reverently in her extended palms, as if she were making an offering to the gods, was a small white box. "Have you seen Jody?" she asked in an anxious voice. "Is Jody up there?"

April remembered that Jody was Talon's handsome young male assistant. He did the nitty-gritty work of running the gallery. "No, and he's not in his own office, either," she supplied helpfully. "We were just down there." Tony ducked his head and made a disgusted, muttering noise in her ear. Something like "Tellthewholeworldwhydon'tcha?"

"He promised to look at my slides."

Tony perked up. "Slides?"

The girl extended the box. "Of my work."

"Slides . . ." Tony repeated searchingly.

Although April's heart had gone out to the young woman, who looked as if she was taking the phrase *starving artist* a little too seriously, they had to be on their way. She made a mental note to look into becoming a patron of the girl's art. "Please excuse us," she said, and grabbed Tony's sleeve so he'd follow.

He pulled up at the second-level landing. "Wait— there's something I've missed. A clue. It's on the tip of my tongue."

"Talon'll be on the tip of your—well, *hi*, Talon!" April said, interrupting herself by invoking the enthusiasm of a beauty contestant. She made a fist so the other woman wouldn't glimpse the digits inscribed on her palm. "We were just checking out the paintings up here. Great show! Really impressive! Absolutely...Daliesque! Magnificent, uh, brushwork." She gritted her teeth, beaming inanely, and rushed Tony down the remaining steps. Silently fuming, Talon stared daggers after them.

"So who'd you get on the phone?" April asked as soon as they'd left the gallery. A light rain had cooled the evening air; she clutched her fringed wrap around her bare shoulders. The wet ebony ribbon of Superior Street shone with blurred watercolor reflections of the city lights. "Was it one of the thugs?"

"Nope, the number belonged to a bar called the Winner's Circle. Out near the racetrack in Arlington."

"Aha," April said with relish. "The thugs' hangout."

"Maybe."

"When are we going to check it out?"

Tony stopped by his car, a dark blue coupe spangled with raindrops. He avoided April's gaze as he unlocked the door. "We aren't."

"Of course we are," she said, climbing into the car after raising the hem of her long dress all the way up to her thighs. She bunched the excess fabric in her lap and peered up at Tony hopefully. His gaze was concentrated on her legs. She crossed them. "How about tomorrow?"

Tony shuttered his eyes, swallowed audibly as he rounded the front bumper by touch, and reopened them only to save himself from walking out into traffic. "Tomorrow ain't never gonna come," he said out of the side of his mouth as he got behind the wheel.

April gloated. When Tony had to resort to tough-guy lingo, she knew he'd landed square in the palm of her hand. "Of course tomorrow will come," she replied, complacent as she unfurled her fist to examine the smeared digits of the Winner's Circle telephone number. *Especially for feisty dames named Lola...*

"THEN YOU REALLY ARE an archaeologist," she said flatly about thirty minutes later.

When Tony winced, April shifted uneasily on the kitchen stool, knowing her sense of sinking disappointment had sounded in her voice. She didn't have anything against archaeology per se. She simply wasn't prepared to surrender her favorite Tony Farentino secret fantasy image so abruptly.

With a tiny sigh she closed her eyes, rested her elbows on the counter, hooked the heels of her sandals over the rungs of the stool and gave it the old college try. She pictured Tony in a pith helmet and khakis instead of a fedora and trench coat. His .38 revolver dissolved into a dinky pickax. Ugh. She added a few pottery shards. *Boring.* Fragmented bones? Maybe a skull? Hmm, getting better. An evil criminal mastermind and a race for a cache of Incan gold? Complicated by cannibals who lurked in the jungle? Not bad!

"Wasn't Indiana Jones an archaeologist?" she murmured. Her eyelids flashed open. "And *he* wore a fedora!"

Tony shook his head and put away his defunct college ID and still-valid National Archaeology Association membership card. "Do you base all your perceptions on the movies?"

"Why not? Works better than reality."

"Having faced a few moments of stark reality myself, I can't completely disagree." He paused significantly. "But I wouldn't have thought the same was true of the woman known as The Madcap Heiress."

April tilted her face up to shake her tousled hair out of it. "Darling Tony, The Madcap Heiress is pure fantasy herself. She's a silly, diverting, convenient persona I've assumed to combat...boredom." She picked up a dainty Sevres china cup and sipped the coffee Godfrey had left for them, wondering why she was confessing the truth—

at least some of it—to Tony when as far as the rest of Chicago was concerned she'd wholeheartedly embraced the very essence of her frivolous public personality. The heiress part was, of course, a given, no matter what reality she chose.

"Let's not be bored, whatever the cost," Tony replied dryly, although he looked intrigued.

She felt compelled to go on. Was it because she wanted him to think better of her? "Like you," she said, "I'm not quite the person I appear to be."

"You're doing a very apt imitation, then."

She glanced around the large, well-equipped kitchen of her town house. Godfrey had been given a free hand in its renovation. He'd invested most of the generous budget in professional-quality appliances like the mammoth restaurant range, convection oven and glass-doored refrigerator. The oak-and-black-tile decor was elegantly plain, without a feminine frill in sight—unlike the rest of the house. She and her P.I.-turned-archaeologist hadn't made it to Monkeyshines; they sat instead at her granite-topped kitchen island with coffee and tiny double-spiral-shaped cookies Godfrey called palmiers.

April shrugged. "It's easy when you have unlimited funds to create the proper settings and costumes."

"Don't forget those proper blue-blooded connections of yours." Tony crunched a palmier between his even white teeth. When he swallowed April saw that his jaw was tight. He cocked an eyebrow. "Or are you hinting that you're not one of the ritzy San Francisco Pierces after all?"

"I'm afraid I am. By marriage."

Tony coughed on cookie crumbs. "You're married?"

April clenched her own jaw. "Widowed."

"Widowed?"

She nodded. The word was so stark and simple when compared to the reality of her marriage at twenty-one to

Freeman Pierce and her gradual realization that his debonair looks, charm and enthusiastic adoration had
masked what was actually a relentless need to control
every aspect of his naive young wife's existence. Still, her
romantic illusions of what marriage should be hadn't died
easily. Although she'd escaped once, early on, her husband had lured her back with seemingly heartfelt profes-
sions of "love."

That first brief flirtation with freedom had resulted in
Freeman obtaining a measure of control over April's income from the Throckmorton family trust fund via a
positively Victorian clause inserted by her chauvinistic
great-grandfather. Freeman had arranged for the money
to be doled out in bimonthly allotments small enough to
preclude further escape attempts—at least well-funded
ones. He hadn't thought her capable of anything less.

Accustomed to being pampered, neither had April. At
first. But she'd made another desperate escape halfway
through her twenty-fourth year, and had surprised even
herself by taking—and holding—a waitressing job to
supplement the income that had gotten her as far as a
small town in Illinois. When Freeman had tracked her
down, she'd staunchly withstood his attempts at recon-
ciliation even though her feet were blistered and her hair
had begun to smell like the deep fat fryers.

April added a dollop of cream to her coffee and
watched as it swirled through the hot Costa Rican blend.
"Freeman Pierce was killed in an airplane accident fifteen months ago," she told Tony, neatly excising the fact
that they'd been officially separated at the time. "Making me a very merry widow."

Tony set his cup in its saucer with a small crash.

"That sounded terrible, didn't it?" Appalled at herself, April put her head in her hands to hide her stricken
face. "I'm sorry, I'm sorry," she whispered. *I'm sorry
that I meant it. And I'm sorry that I couldn't mourn my*

husband because the bald truth was that his death meant my ultimate freedom.

"I'm sorry, too."

Tony's voice was as smooth as the cream in her coffee. It swirled through her, warm and kind and understanding, even though she hadn't explained her cold-blooded statement. He'd seemed to know anyway...

She looked up, surprisingly soothed, though she once again wordlessly swallowed her remorse. "You see, my marriage was not a happy one. And the Pierces were not pleased when I departed just a few days after the funeral instead of staying to observe what they'd deemed an appropriately lengthy and subdued period of mourning." Not to mention the fact that they'd coveted, on the theory that one can never be too wealthy, Freeman's insurance money and the multimillion dollar settlement she'd eventually been awarded by the airline as "compensation" for her husband's death.

"First I flew to Europe to visit my parents. My father amuses himself by writing travel articles for upscale magazines, and they happened to be in the south of France. Although they tried to comfort me, they couldn't fix what was wrong. I went back to the family cottage in Maine. My younger sister and Grandmother Throckmorton did their best, but that didn't work, either. I still felt out of place."

"So you came to Chicago," Tony stated in measured tones.

"Yes," April said with a sigh. "I'd lived briefly in the state, but I didn't really know anyone in Chicago. I had decided it was best if I discarded the past."

"You became The Madcap Heiress."

"Do you think I'm awful?" She tried to ask the question in a flippant way, but the truth was that it went to the heart of what she'd asked of herself every day since her husband's death. How disrespectful was a widow who hadn't shed a tear? How awful was she for wanting to rid herself of the settlement money as quickly as possible? And, even worse, by spending much of it in ways that would have made Freeman's blood boil?

"I think..." Tony said slowly, making her await his judgment in breathless suspense while his eyes searched hers. "I think there's a lot more to April Pierce than what she allows most people to see." He glanced down at his hands, resting on the polished stone countertop. "And also more to your motives...?"

Was he referring to the unconventional way she'd commemorated her late, lamented marriage? Or to the search for Dunky? She hadn't been entirely forthright about either one, but the prospect of confessing every itty-bitty detail was daunting.

Time to turn the tables.

"Well, *I* think this subject is a dreadful bore!" she said with a sudden vehemence, using her spoiled deb voice. "Let's analyze your motives instead, shall we? How was it that you came to be masquerading as a private investigator?" She laughed and batted her lashes coquettishly, as was her fallback habit. "Not that you haven't been doing an extremely apt imitation, my darling Tony. In fact, it's been so apt I'm not sure you've yet convinced me otherwise."

Slanting a teasing gaze up at him, she fiddled with the plate of cookies. "Say something archaeological."

He scowled. "Is this a test?"

Unconcerned, she nodded and licked flecks of sugar off her fingertips.

There was a long pause before he spoke. "Should I tell you about the scent of the burning rain forest and the sounds of the latest civil war's mortar fire in the distance? How to decipher glyphs? Describe the gory applications of an ancient culture's various bloodletting instruments? Should I tell you what it's like to discover a stela, to be the first man in two thousand years to look upon the face of an ancient Maya warrior king?''

April's eyes widened at the intensity of his voice. His gaze was riveted to hers but she wasn't certain what he was seeing. A steamy jungle scene drifted into her own imagination, lushly green and shadowed, populated only by a black-haired man with vividly dark eyes. He was stripped to the waist, his torso rippling with brown sweat-slickened muscles as he held out his upturned hand. *"Come to me, Stella,"* he whispered.

She blinked in consternation. "Who's this Stella person?"

The shallow dimple in Tony's cheek deepened when he smiled. "A stela is a carved stone monument."

"Is that what you were working on in Guatemala?"

"It was a part of the Cayaxechun site, but I'd moved on to a burial tomb that had been discovered nearby. We'd tunneled through twenty-five feet of bedrock and were about to enter the chamber when the earthquake hit."

"That would be enough to turn anyone into a private investigator!"

He laughed regretfully. "I didn't mean that literally, although if it had happened a few hours later, we might have been entombed ourselves."

April, whose adventures had always been more silly than dangerous, shuddered at the thought. "And the site was demolished?"

"There was some damage. I felt fortunate that no one had been badly injured." He picked up his cup, the floral-patterned porcelain looking fragile in his roughened brown hands. April noticed with a small zing to the heart that his fingers were deft and gentle in handling the china. He wouldn't drop it. He wouldn't break it.

"The tomb took the worst of it," Tony continued. His eyes had gone a flat mud brown. "A large section had collapsed in on itself." She made consoling sounds; he shrugged with manly aplomb. "So that was that. It was the close of the season, my team's funding had run out, I returned to Chicago to raise more money and found instead that I'd been denied tenure. It seemed the powers-that-be preferred a play-it-safe textbook epigraphist whose family had endowed a chair to a disaster-prone archaeologist who'd spent more time in South America than in the classroom of late. Can't say as I blame them."

"Well, I can," April sniffed. "The low-down dirty dogs!" Then she tilted her head thoughtfully. "Exactly how much does it cost to endow a chair?"

For an instant Tony's expression hovered between insult and disdain, but then his eyes warmed, the skin at the corners crinkling with his smile. "Well, that's very generous, ma'am, but you can forget it. I'm not interested in buying myself a professorship. And you've already endowed, so to speak, my swivel chair at Farentino Investigations. Providing you haven't decided to take Donkey's case elsewhere now that you know the truth."

"As if I would! Your work has been exemplary even if you aren't licensed. I might be flighty, but I'm not disloyal and I'm not a quitter." She felt pleased with this dashing declaration until she remembered the marriage from which she'd cut and run. She'd never cheated on Freeman—even when the only feelings he'd evoked in her were frustration and fear—but she *had* quit. Her husband and then the rest of the stiff-necked Pierces had been merciless in pointing out how she'd tarnished their sterling family reputation.

"Donkey is lucky to have a friend like you, April," said Tony.

His words bolstered her confidence. "Donkey—that is, Dunky—has been a very good friend to me since I moved to Chicago. All you know of him is his addiction to gambling, but he's also sweet and talented and funny. He flunked out of business school, but he loves to paint, eat chocolate éclairs and read murder mysteries and Victorian erotica. Sometimes all at once.''

April paused, smiling at a memory of Dunky, roly-poly in his quilted satin smoking jacket, rhapsodizing over the genius of Fogbottom's skin tones. "Despite his flaws, he's easily the best of the Dunkingtons." Unstated but hopefully readily apparent was the fact that though her loyal attachment to Dunky was protective and sisterly, it was not in the least romantic. "Arthur Dunkington is of the old school—he thinks his son is a useless wastrel, probably off on another of his sprees. Dunky's mother, Sugar, is kinder, but she goes along with whatever MacArthur decrees. And you met Talon.''

"Yes, I met Talon.'' Tony suddenly put his hands over April's, laying them flat, covering her smaller hands from fingertip to wrist. It was an uncommon gesture, yet surprisingly effective if the tingling of her scalp meant anything. She twined her legs tightly around the stool when he began stroking her wrists with feather-light fingertips. She wasn't feeling the least bit sisterly.

"After that phone call, she not only tops the list of suspects, she *is* the list," Tony added.

What? Who? April wondered foggily. Ah, yes, Talon, the Cruella De Vil of the art world. "Don't forget the thugs," she said, perfectly willing to do so for the moment.

Tony slid his thumbs and index fingers around her wrists like bracelets and still managed to carry on a straight conversation. "At least we know that if the thugs have been hired by Talon and not her brother's bookie, they're only after the painting. Donkey won't get hurt even if they find him before we do.''

"Mmm-hmm.'' April leaned forward. If Tony's gaze lowered to the drooping neckline of her dress, she didn't notice. She was too busy trying to figure out if the pulsating sensation flowing through their hands was coming from his fingertips, the veins in her wrists, or perhaps a source more emotional than it was physiological.

Tony also leaned forward. "I want you to promise that you won't go near the thugs, April." He touched his lips to hers briefly. "Promise."

"It's not fair, kissing me like that and asking—"

"Oh, sorry." He interrupted her, a hint of laughter in his voice. "How about if I kiss you like this instead?" With his hands again covering hers like warm suede gloves, he gently flicked his tongue across her bottom lip, then slid it along the slick underside of the upper with a tantalizing promise. She shivered and parted her lips, her head tilting in synchronization with his as they kissed as though other kisses had been simply practice for the real thing. Other kisses? April thought dazedly. Had there been other kisses? Certainly none like Tony's!

By the time he broke away, she was thoroughly undone. "Okay," she said, managing to sound droll even though she was quite serious, "kiss me like *that* and I'll do anything you want."

"You do promise, then?"

A huge breath shuddered through her. Tony was so disarmingly handsome in a tux, even if it was only a rental. His hair gleamed blue-black under the fluorescents and his bow tie was undone, the formal white shirt unbuttoned enough for her to see the smooth brown skin of his strong throat, the ridge of his collarbone, a few wisps of curling black hair...rats, she was a goner.

She crossed her heart with her right hand and held up the left. "April Marie-Therese Throckmorton Fairchild Pierce swears she will not confront any nasty old thugs without darling Mr. Farentino's by-your-leave."

Tony still seemed doubtful. Godfrey clumped into the kitchen, looking immensely thuggish in tattoos and black leather. He took one look at the infatuated expression on April's face, another at the macho-male-protective thing going on in Tony's, and glanced at the telephone number scrawled across her upraised palm.

"Juvenile," he snorted. He took a liter of bottled water out of the refrigerator. "Get yourselves some little black books, why don'tcha?" He made a noise that sounded like something between a grunt and a chuckle, and clumped out of the room.

Tony turned back to April. "One day you'll have to tell me exactly what it is you see in that man."

5

The Lady and the Thugs

"YOU DON'T WANT TO BE messing around with thugs, Tony. Your momma would fricassee my carcass if her only son got injured while working for Farentino Investigations."

Tony rolled his eyes at the voice booming through the telephone in his hand. "I'm thirty-four, Uncle Rocco. I've been through a civil war, an earthquake and a tenure hearing. Don't tell Mom, but I bet I can also survive two hired thugs."

"'Scuse me if I don't make book on that, boy." Rocco chuckled.

"The odds are on my side," Tony said, mildly affronted. "That thug talking on the phone to Talon last night sounded as dumb as a stump and twice as knotheaded."

"You might have the brains, but they got the firepower. Say this Donkey-boy is in real deep with a loan shark. I guaran-damn-tee they ain't gonna bother fooling around if they think you've got information they want." The murmuring sounds of the casino could be heard in the background when Rocco paused ominously. "Steer clear, Tony."

"I may not have that choice."

Rocco groaned. "What's she look like?"

"Who?"

"The skirt. The dame. The broad."

"I didn't mention a woman."

A hearty guffaw thundered over the line. "You can't fool Uncle Rocco. In a situation like this, there's always a dame."

"Well, this dame is incredibly naive. And, unfortunately, she's got more daring than what's good for her."

"Blond?"

"How'd you know?"

"We Mediterranean types always get it bad for the blondes."

"I don't—" Tony started to protest, then stopped. Actually, the truth was he *did*. The odds of April fitting into his life—and vice versa—were as likely as Rocco making it out of Vegas without losing his shirt, but, yeah, Tony had it bad anyway. He was in deep, and getting deeper all the time.

"I don't plan to have it out with the thugs," he said instead to Rocco. "I'll just hang around the Winner's Circle and see what I can learn."

"Loser's Circle, more like. The place is a dive."

"You know it well, then?"

"Every gambler north of Churchill Downs knows it well. Give Stumps, the bartender, my name and maybe he'll decide not to toss you out on your freakin' famous I.Q."

"I'll wear a helmet," Tony promised. Maybe he'd also take Godfrey, as April had suggested.

Rocco harrumphed. "So's how business? Miss Estelle put you in your place yet?"

"Speaking of blondes..."

"Miss Estelle is a blonde? Can't say as I'd ever noticed." Rocco's bluster didn't quite ring true.

"I get the feeling she'd gladly turn me over to the thugs if that meant she could have you all to herself again."

Rocco spat a shocked expletive. "Hell's bells, where'd you get that idea, Tony?" he roared. "What did she say?"

"Oh, you know Miss Estelle. She's maintaining her cool. But, I dunno…something about the way she's been going at the word processor makes me think she's redirecting lascivious thoughts into a more productive outlet." This pronouncement was met with an uncharacteristic silence. Tony was glad his uncle was hundreds of miles away and couldn't see the teasing nature of his nephew's expression.

"You—you're joshing me, now, boy," Rocco finally sputtered. "Ain'tcha?"

"What do you think?"

"I think I hear the dice at the craps table calling my name."

"You sure that's not Miss Estelle's love song?" Tony asked, and laughed out loud when Rocco slammed down the telephone on another emphatic burst of four-letter words. A clear-cut case of protesting too much, Tony decided. Who'd've suspected?

The intercom buzzed. "A Ms. April Pierce to see you, Mr. Farentino," announced Miss Estelle. A shade of accusation crept into her voice. "I have no such appointment noted in my book, however."

"Why don't we play it by ear, Miss Estelle?"

She, too, harrumphed, making it clear she had no intention of relaxing her habitual discipline on his say-so. "Shall I send Ms. Pierce in?"

"Do that," Tony said, bounding out from behind the desk to open the office door. Instead of waiting on the threshold, as eager to see him as he was to see her, April was bent over Miss Estelle's desk, spraying the inside of the secretary's wrist with perfume. "Sniff," she said.

Miss Estelle's face was as screwed up as a snarl of government red tape. She held her arm out straight from the shoulder and sniffed the air tentatively. One eye opened, then the other. She rubbed her wrists together and sniffed again.

"Heavenly, isn't it?" April cooed. She started to put the flacon back into her tiny velvet and lace reticule, then changed her mind and placed it on the secretary's desk. "Two-fifty an ounce and worth every cent."

"April, what are you doing here?" Tony asked before he could be treated to the sight of Miss Estelle attempting girl talk.

"I was on my way to what I'm sure will be an extremely dull garden party. I decided to stop by to check when you're planning to go to Arlington. Did you think I'd let you investigate the Winner's Circle without me?"

"You promised," he said reproachfully. "Besides, you look like Mary Poppins. From what Rocco told me this place is a scuzzy racetrack dive. You'd never blend in wearing an outfit like that." April was wearing a pretty-girl green print dress with leg-of-mutton sleeves. Also white leather button boots, a petticoat and a wide-brimmed straw hat. The ensemble made Miss Estelle's cardigan and cameo look even more sensible than usual.

April widened her sea green eyes *du jour* and surprised him by saying, "You're absolutely right."

"Okay, then, I'm leaving now—but not for Arlington. I've got...other plans. They don't include you." Tony thought it best to make as clean and quick a getaway as possible—before she could have another of her disastrous brainstorms. "Remember, you promised," he said as he opened the door.

April put her foot up on the secretary's desk. "Go on, Tony," she said, waving him unconcernedly out the door. "Do your manly-man things. I'll just stick around to visit with Miss Estelle. Maybe she can help me do up the rest of these teensy little buttons on my boots. Godfrey was no use at all—there are too many steroids in his fingertips."

Tony hovered in the hallway. When he looked back past the open door, Miss Estelle was busily buttonhooking April's boot, gazing up at her with a dawning mixture of shock and—could it be?—admiration. "Don't even think of following me," he warned, but neither of them seemed to hear. April hunched over and whispered to Miss Estelle, showing the secretary something in the palm of her hand.

THE WINNER'S CIRCLE was all that a racetrack dive should be. Conveniently located near the Arlington International Racetrack so unlucky bettors could drown their sorrow without delay, it boasted four televisions, one for each corner of the large, square room, and an equal number of pool tables. Most of the light in the bar came from the shaded lamps hung low over the pool tables, illuminating the green felt but consigning the rest of the room to an eternal dingy gloom. Tony, playing pool with an ex-and-probably-future-con who was about to relieve him of another five bucks, didn't immediately notice April's entrance into the murk.

She slithered up to the darkest side of the bar, sticking to the shadows and being as unobtrusive as a leggy blonde in a white leatherette miniskirt, ankle-high button boots and a tight red off-the-shoulder top could be. Which wasn't very, she immediately saw. *C'est la vie.* She hadn't really expected otherwise.

She sat. The stools on either side of her were immediately taken by two guys, one ponytailed and sleazy, the other zip-cut and chunky. They wafted lust-provoked pheromones that blended badly with the miasma of stale cigarette smoke, cheap liquor and rank fried food. *Eau de* dive bar, April thought, breathing through her mouth. A gray-haired bartender missing three fingers on his right hand—who knew about the left?—brought her a beer. The sleazeball next to her offered to pay.

"Thanks a million," she simpered. "My name's Lola."

He leered. "People call me Lucky, and now I know why."

April giggled and fluffed her bouffant with freshly applied glittery glue-on nails. Two armfuls of neon-colored plastic bracelets slid to her elbows with a rattle. "Are you lucky in love or lucky at the track?"

"Both," he boasted, waving at the bartender for a refill. He peeled another bill off a money-clipped stash that might've been impressive to anyone but an heiress.

"Oooh," April squealed, "T-Bone told me I'd meet some nifty guys at the Winner's Circle."

The chunky guy on her right lifted his bottle out of a sticky pool of spilled beer and clinked it hard against his teeth. April winced. "You a friend of T-Bone's?" he slurred, setting the bottle back on the bar. Sideways. The dregs of his beer trickled out.

"Uh-huh." April nodded, peering ineffectually into the dull, carcinogenic haze hanging thickly in the air. "Is he here?"

"Over to the juke."

Her gaze followed the wobble of her stoolmate's pointing finger. A huge man, probably six-five with muscles to match, was draped over the jukebox, smoking desultorily. The juke's multicolored lights intermittently washed over a face that fit his name—red and beefy. April instantly recognized him as one of the thugs. No surprise there. "I should go and say hi."

Lucky handcuffed her wrist. "Don't run off so soon, Lola, baby. You haven't finished that beer I paid for."

Finished? She hadn't even started. April slid off the stool. "How about I play you a song?" she coaxed with an intimate smile, easing her hand away from his with another rattle of her bracelets. "Do you know the one about *L-O-L-A,* Lo-la?" she singsonged, edging away. "L-O-L-A—"

"Low-la-aah," Lucky crooned obligingly. "Hurry back now." The smarminess of his smile oozed across her skin. "Don't forget."

She blew him a kiss. "Impossible." *At least until I've bathed in disinfectant.* Rummaging in her pocketbook as she wove past a table of bleary-eyed racetrack grooms, she found a pair of sequined cat's-eye sunglasses that would do as a further disguise in case T-Bone might recognize her. Almost blind once they were in place, she stumbled past various tables and chairs until she bumped into the jukebox and something huge and sweaty and male.

Her progress had not gone undetected. In the middle of losing a game to a wiry guy called Eldridge who just happened to have a scar bisecting his upper lip, Tony looked up and squinted through the smoke. His face went white, then red. He banked the seven ball so hard it almost jumped off the table.

"Oops, sorry," April said to T-Bone. "It's dark in here, isn't it?"

"Stumps painted out thuh windows."

She let fly with another girlish giggle. It was sort of fun being a floozy. "My guess is Stumps is the bartender."

"How'dja know?" T-Bone said, crushing the butt of another cigarette into an overflowing ashtray.

April decided T-Bone was running extremely low in the wattage department. She took a quarter out of her purse and studied the song list. "What did you say your name was?"

He looked a little confused. Definitely a dim bulb, she affirmed. "T-Bone," he answered. "Like thuh steak."

"Gee, does *everyone* in this place have a nickname?" April smiled prettily, tilting her head as she tried to make out T-Bone's features through the dark glasses so she could commit them to memory. One never knew when one might be faced with a police lineup. "I'm only called Lola, but I have friends named Ju-Ju and Sistie, and another named after a bird's claws..." She let her voice trail off, hoping he might supply Talon's name.

"See that guy?" he asked instead. April, turning, got a glimpse out of the side of her glasses of the other weasely thug. Also of Tony, in faded jeans, a ripped Harley-Davidson T-shirt and an early five-o'clock shadow. He was chalking a pool stick and glaring at her. She whipped back to face the jukebox, pretending she hadn't noticed.

"He swears there's a town in Iowa named after him," T-Bone continued. He lit a match on his fingernail and touched it to the end of the cigarette hanging out the corner of his mouth. "You ever hear of a town in Iowa name of Eldridge?"

"Gee, I don't know." After sneaking another peek at Tony, April blew out the match before the flame reached T-Bone's fingers. "But if there is, I'd say Eldridge was named after the town, not the other way around." She started punching buttons at random, the back of her neck flushing under the intensity of Tony's angry stare.

"Yeah, that sounds right. You're awful smart." T-Bone was apparently easily impressed.

"Oh, I know lots about all kinds of stuff. Cosmetology, fashion merchandising, telemarketing. I even studied art by correspondence course."

This time, T-Bone took the bait. "You ever hear of an artist name of Ello Fogbottom?"

April tensed. Ello? Oh, *L.O.* Lesley Orville Fogbottom. She'd struck gold! Or, perhaps, taking into account Eldridge's slicked-back ducktail, *oil.*

"Um, I think so," she said to T-Bone. "He's some old dude, right? Probably his paintings are worth a fortune."

"He's not just old. He's dead. Eldridge says that's thuh best thing for an artist to be."

The jukebox was playing a crooning cowboy's love song. The click of pool balls drew April's attention. Tony was so mad he'd apparently forgotten to lose. He was knocking balls into pockets with icy precision, scarcely bothering to take his eyes off her to line up the shots. Eldridge's scar puckered as he inhaled, slitty-eyed, then blasted the table with two lungfuls of acrid cigarillo smoke. Tony coughed once, aimed through the haze and sank the eight ball in a side pocket.

Uh-oh. "Don't tell me you own a genuine Fogbottom?" April said quickly to T-Bone. He took her haste as greedy enthusiasm. "A masterpiece!" she gushed. "Wow, I'm impressed!"

He puffed up. "I know a woman who sells them, and me and Eldridge—"

A strong male hand circled April's upper arm. "Let's get out of here." She turned to see Tony glowering down at her, his eyes hot enough to scald. "Now," he ordered through gritted teeth.

"No, not now," she said, without bothering to sound ditzy. She didn't like being manhandled, and especially not at such an inconvenient moment. She turned back to T-Bone and laid her free hand over his thick wrist, fastidiously avoiding the ashtray and blatantly ignoring Tony. "Tell me more, T-Bone."

Tony slid his left arm around her waist, effortlessly hoisted her off her feet and turned her in midair so she was aimed at the door. "Yes," he hissed into her ear, *"now."* He shrugged at T-Bone. "Sorry. My wife doesn't always do as she's told."

April's head jerked up. She'd sworn that no one would ever talk about her like that again, not even in jest! She wiggled helplessly against Tony's vise of a grip, then steeled her conscience and back-kicked, stabbing the sharp heel of one of her boots into the bony part of his shin. Although his knee buckled, he didn't drop her.

T-Bone rose to full height. "I don't think Lola wants to go home witchoo." He plucked April out of Tony's arms—she felt Tony tighten his hold momentarily, then let go when it was clearly either that or a tug-of-war—and plopped her into a nearby chair. "You shouldn't treat a lady like that."

Tony glanced at the Lola getup scornfully. "That ain't no lady."

T-Bone reared back and slugged him in the gut with the mighty force of a pile driver. April winced as Tony staggered backward, air whooshing from his lungs. She clambered up onto the chair, looking for her spot. Maybe Tony was acting like a Neanderthal, but he was *her* Neanderthal!

With a bloodcurdling howl April launched herself off the chair. Eldridge rushed into the fray waving a pool cue. She landed with a whump on his back instead of T-Bone's, and immediately slid right off again, her hands slithering through his greasy hair. "Yuck," she said, and landed on her bottom on the carpet among a litter of peanut shells, cigarette stubs and crushed potato chips.

"Hey, that's my woman," screeched Lucky, shooting himself off his bar stool. "I saw her first!" He swung wildly at Eldridge, who ducked. The blow bounced off a wall of bulging pecs. When T-Bone glanced down as if to flick away a pesky mosquito, Tony's roundhouse right slammed with a thud into his eye instead of his jaw. T-Bone, having the reaction time one might expect of a slab of meat, staggered against the jukebox and put one massive hand up to his face.

"Jeez, you hit me," he said dully.

Everyone stopped to stare.

Tony snatched a pool cue out of an onlooker's hands and brandished it like a rapier. Quick as a mongoose, Eldridge dodged forward, stabbing his cue at Tony's face. Tony sidestepped and with a lethal whistle of displaced air swiped his stick past Eldridge's ribs, purposely missing by no more than an eighth of an inch. Eldridge sucked in his stomach, his cue clattering to the floor.

"Nobody move," Tony snarled. He hooked his fingers in the back of April's waistband and yanked her off the floor in one smooth motion.

"Jeez, you hit me," T-Bone repeated. He prodded his swelling eye socket and moaned. Lucky and Eldridge ogled the expanse of bare thigh showing beneath the hem of April's rucked-up skirt.

She twitched it down. "I can walk," she snapped at Tony, and marched to the door as if that had been her plan all along. Cautiously Tony followed, keeping his back to the exit and the sharp end of the cue weaving.

Stumps stood calmly behind the bar, polishing pilsners with a neat twist of his two remaining fingers. "Rocco's gonna love this one." He chuckled.

Acknowledging the bartender with a nod, Tony left the pool stick propped by the door. *"Sheeee-it!"* April heard Eldridge swear as she stepped outside and sucked in a breath of the marvelously fresh air. "That was the Pierce woman. Dunkington's girlfriend! Move it, T-Bone, we gotta follow her to his hideout—"

Tony slammed the door. April was already climbing into her convertible, keys in hand, by the time he caught up to her. He vaulted into the passenger seat and issued a one-word command as she started the engine. "Drive."

Thin-lipped, April backed out and zipped over to Tony's car. T-Bone and Eldridge burst out of the Winner's Circle. "What are you waiting for?" Tony demanded. He thumped his fist on the back of her headrest. "Go. Drive. Now."

"I do not take commands like a good little doggy," she said, ice in her tone. "Drive yourself home, Tony. I don't want you in my car."

He stared, dumbfounded, and didn't move. A lumbering T-Bone loomed in the side-view mirror, appearing very close indeed despite the printed warning. "Oh, blast it anyway," April said, and stepped on the gas, cutting the steering wheel hard to the right. The back wheels spit gravel into T-Bone's face.

She easily left the thugs in the dust by breaking the speed limit with flinty aplomb, then doubling back once they hit downtown Arlington. She wanted to drop Tony at the Winner's Circle, but he said he valued his life more than his car. He'd pick it up later. Neither of them spoke again until they were on the expressway to Chicago, cruising at the speed limit this time. The wind was flattening April's bouffant. She spit a strand of it out of her mouth, the taste of hair spray tart on her tongue. "I am not an obedient pet," she seethed in a low voice. "I am not your child. Or your *wife.*"

"Thank God," snapped Tony, slumped in the bucket seat.

"You had no right to treat me like that!"

His head whipped around. "I got you out of a bad situation. You might thank me!"

She blinked back tears of what she decided was pure rage. "Thank you? Hah! I should have left you to T-Bone!"

"Unlike you, I could have held my own."

"Oh, yeah, you were doing a great job. If I hadn't tackled Eldridge, you'd be sporting a pool cue through the spleen."

Tony was staring straight ahead now, his face grim. "And *you'd* be that ponytailed slime-bucket's trophy."

"I was just fine until you decided to manhandle me like a sack of potatoes," she protested, her voice edging toward tremulous. She gritted her teeth.

Tony glanced sideways. "April," he said more reasonably, "I had to get you out of there."

"Right when T-Bone was spilling his guts," she wailed. "He was about to tell me about his connection to Talon and you ruined it!"

"Well, excuse me, but I wasn't the one who broke my promise."

Her grip on the wheel tightened as she blinked furiously. "I didn't break my promise. Exactly."

"Oh, no?"

"I said April Marie-Therese Throckmorton Fairchild Pierce wouldn't consort with the thugs. I didn't say anything about Lola." It was a weak argument and she knew it. She was mad and frustrated and she was wrong. Which made her even angrier.

"Semantics," Tony sniped in an aggravating way.

Just like a man, April thought. Just like a typical, bossy, know-it-all man! She clamped her lips together to stop herself from screeching like a fishwife—although even that was better than crying—and concentrated on the road. She zipped the convertible around a semi doing seventy.

"Slow down," Tony said. "Be reasonable for once in your life. You shouldn't be driving—"

"Of course not. I should let *you* drive, I suppose?"

"I was going to say it's not safe to drive when you're in such a temper." He heaved a tired sigh, muttering beneath his breath. It sounded to April as though he'd said, "Temper *tantrum*."

She knew she was reacting badly. She also knew why, and Tony didn't. But she wasn't in the mood to explain that his cavalier manner in ordering her around had brought back the worst of her memories of her late husband—the memories she'd been trying to banish any way she could. And maybe that was why she'd broken her promise to Tony, she realized. If she never obeyed, she'd never again be controlled.

Nonetheless, she eased her foot off the accelerator, enough to slow the convertible's speed, but not so much that Tony would think she was obeying his command.

Simmering with contrariness, she peeked at him from the corner of her eye. He was sitting on his spine, his long denim-clad legs folded within the close space of the front seat so his knees were almost level with his chin. With his disreputable black T-shirt, sexy stubbled jaw and glowering brow, he was the very image of a bad boy. The irrepressible Lola was getting turned on. April was, too, even though she was definitely still mad at him. Maybe what they said about the connection between anger and passion was true....

Then April reminded herself of her marriage to Freeman, and took her treacherous hormones back in hand.

She was determined not to make the same mistake twice. Even though she knew that Tony was probably only a Neanderthal in disguise, and that he'd had her best interests at heart, she couldn't be sure that the way he'd treated her at the Winner's Circle was only an instinctive reaction to danger. After all, Freeman Pierce had seemed like an upstanding sort, too, and look how wrong she'd been about *him*.

So, no, she would not forgive Tony for manhandling her! Not when she had just as much a right to investigate the Winner's Circle as he did. He was her private eye, not her bodyguard. He was her employee, not her boss.

Never again would she allow others to tell her what to do. She would not sit quietly, obey her elders, school her impulses.

She would *not* be reasonable!

6

Slip-sliding Away

TWO DAYS LATER, Tony was summoned to April's town house. He was to have an audience with the princess herself at eleven a.m. on the dot.

The command was issued via Godfrey, and Tony growled with bad temper as he slammed Rocco's phone down, just as disgusted with himself as with Miss High-and-Mighty. He'd wanted to keep their dealings businesslike, and now he was going to get exactly what he'd asked for. Great.

At first Tony fully intended to make April wait a good long time before he put in an appearance, but by eleven o'clock he couldn't withstand another second of Miss Estelle's dour, knowing silence. He decided that he might as well go on over to Palace Circle to take The Madcap Heiress down a notch.

Traffic was snarled and slow; he had plenty of time to cool off before reaching the lake breezes of April's million-dollar view. Stomping up the stone steps, trying to work himself back into a lather, Tony instead found himself puzzling over why April had reacted so strongly to the incident at the racetrack bar in the first place. He'd thought he was rescuing her from harm, but she'd bared her glitter nails and hissed at his offer of protection as if she were a wildcat in a cage. She'd actually *kicked* him.

His shin had been black-and-blue for two days and was now turning lovely shades of yellow and red.

An attempt at a grimace turned into a grin. Damn, she was feisty.

And he was glad of it, Tony admitted as he twirled the doorbell, glad because it gave him reason to believe there was more to April than the madcap princess persona. Which in turn made it difficult for him to think of her as only a client—even when she was playing the power games of a snippy little spoiled brat.

Such an attitude should've been enough to make him walk away from her. Perhaps he was getting too caught up in this P.I. game, but he couldn't make himself do that. Not when he still hadn't solved the mystery of April Marie-Therese Throckmorton Fairchild Pierce, a.k.a. Lola Peacock.

Tony rang again, more eagerly, and finally the door was opened by Godfrey, frightfully natty in pleated gray linen trousers and a button-down shirt. Lacking his usual scowl, his tattoos discreetly covered, the butler appeared almost normal. Tony was discomfited. When the Pierce homestead turned ordinary, of all things, a smart private eye would be sure to stay on his toes.

Without a word, Godfrey led Tony upstairs. It took Tony ten stairs to figure out what was wrong, then the remainder to contain his amazement. Godfrey was gliding, not clumping! What had April done to him?

"Mr. Farentino to see you, mum," Godfrey announced at the door with an obsequious little nod, his accent as British as crumpets, albeit crumbly crumpets.

Tony, hovering, heard a hasty, whispered confab, an unfamiliar titter, then April's haughtiest voice. "What are you waiting for, Godfrey? Please show him in."

The butler ushered Tony inside the bedroom. April was once again holding court from amidst the plump cushions of her thronelike four-poster, a golden-haired Pom·

eranian with a jeweled collar tucked under her left arm. At her other side was a fair-haired milkmaid type with peaches-and-cream skin and placid doe eyes, her sensible loafers kicked off and her sturdy legs curled among the pillows. The dog yipped; the woman smiled.

Tony saluted. "Tony Farentino reporting for duty."

April did a grande dame nod, then made introductions with a careful composure. "Eve, this is Mr. Tony Farentino, my hired pickax." The two women looked at each other and snickered. "Mr. Farentino, this is Lady Eve Beamish, my best friend in all England. And all U.S. of A., as well." They laughed again, but this time Tony could see that April was only putting on another one of her acts. Although her nose was in the air, her eyes shifted to glance at him from beneath her lashes, waiting for his reaction.

He decided to put aside his pique at being summoned and take a stab at gallantry. It had to go over better than the bully act he'd pulled the other day. He stepped up to the dais, bowed at the waist, took Lady Eve's hand in his and kissed the top lightly. "Please call me Tony."

"And you may call me ... Lady Eve," Lady Eve said, and exchanged a wink and a smile with April.

Tony stepped back, keenly aware of the two friends' amusement and the lingering Godfrey's glower. At least the sparkle was back in April's eyes. He peered, hoping she hadn't had time for her contacts this morning. Nope, her eyes were now lavender. She must sleep in the darned things.

"Lady Eve and I were roommates at Miss Fibbing-White's, a boarding school nestled among the pastoral beauties of Shropshire."

"Dreadful bore," said Lady Eve.

"There will always be an England," April intoned to more muffled laughter and whispered rejoinders. Another inside joke, he assumed. Perhaps in all her jollity

April had already forgotten the episode at the Winner's Circle.

Possibly not. Lady Eve rose from the bed and smoothed her linen walking shorts. "Pleasure to meet you, Tony," she said, stepping into her loafers. "I'm off to search the city for a proper brand of British tea. That Lemon Zingy stuff Godfrey served yesterday will not do." The butler wilted. "You'll take me, won't you, Godfrey?" she coaxed. He blossomed. "There's the boy."

Tony watched them leave, Lady Eve brisk, Godfrey puppy-dog plaintive. "Was it something I said?"

"Something I said," replied April, spoiling her hauteur by making kissy-faced moues at the dog. She chucked it under the jaw. "Lady Eve despises tea. She prefers coffee."

"It looks like Godfrey has a crush on her. Is Lady Eve the type to care that he's *b-a-l-d?*"

The corners of April's mouth twitched, but she ducked her head to concentrate on the preening Pomeranian. "I told her we needed a moment alone," she confessed with a slight frown as she stroked her fingers through the dog's silky fur.

Tony cleared his throat and blurted, "I—I'm sorry, April."

She looked wary. "Pardon?"

He gritted his teeth. He hadn't meant to apologize since he couldn't see that he'd done anything to warrant it. Except for being overly familiar with a client, he supposed, which was something he might regret but would forever remember with pleasure.

"Look," he said, "I suppose it's possible that I was too abrupt with you at the Winner's Circle, ordering you around like I did, but—"

Although there was an air of cautious friendliness about April, she hadn't entirely relented. Her lashes fluttered even as her shoulders stiffened. "You treated me abominably."

"I was protecting you."

"I didn't need—"

"Just like you were protecting me when you jumped on top of Eldridge."

"—rescuing," April finished. "What did you say?"

"You heard me."

Nervously April threaded her fingers around the dog's rhinestone collar. "So it was a mutual thing," she said slowly. "We were a team, of sorts. I hadn't thought of it that way." Patting the bed, she tried a tentative smile. "Sit down, Tony...please?"

Grateful of the offer because he was suddenly feeling unsteady on his feet, Tony sat, sinking several inches into the down-filled duvet. What the hell? he wondered. April's small smile and even smaller overture were apparently big enough to produce a deep, giddy warmth inside him, a warmth that felt strangely like...

Like love.

Uh-oh.

April was staring at him, her expression still mixed, but softening. Not caring to be ignored, the dog nudged its nose up the loose sleeve of her lavender lace peignoir, sniffed the trimming of marabou feathers and sneezed explosively. Both Tony and April flinched, breaking the moment.

A small laugh hiccuped out of April, hinting at her relief. "Oh, poor Asta," she crooned, picking up the dog and cradling it in her lap. "Mama will be back soon, baby."

As Tony watched, his mouth curved into a wry smile. He'd never imagined falling in love with a woman who baby-talked to dogs. Or, for that matter, a woman who changed eye colors as often as she changed clothes and could chat up thugs as smoothly as she handled snooty art snobs. An attraction of opposites, he decided, wondering uneasily what that boded for the future. It made for great chemistry, but what about commitment?

Whoa. He was getting ahead of himself, there. Better to return to the case. "You have to remember that the thugs aren't playing a game, April. They might have gotten violent."

"I suppose you're right," she conceded, then mercurially switched moods. "Actually, things did get violent, didn't they? And you committed yourself admirably." She leaned over Asta to squeeze Tony's biceps, giving him a wide-eyed, you-big-tough-man look. "You're more than a hired pickax. You're muscle."

He grinned. "Yeah, me and T-Bone."

"Poor T-Bone. I'm afraid his weakest muscle is the one between his ears. The medulla oblongata, you know."

"I know."

"Of course you do. But I studied anatomy, too, Tony. I haven't been a Lola all my life."

"Certainly not."

She played with Asta's golden ears. "Are you laughing at me?"

"If I'm laughing, it's only to keep from crying. I'm scared to death of what *your* medulla oblongata will come up with next."

April pretended to pout. "So you are laughing at me!"

Then they both laughed, but Tony sobered quickly. "This isn't funny. It isn't. Do you understand that the only reason I manhandled you was because I feared for your safety?" He brushed his hand across her cheek. "All I could think of was getting you out of that bar. I wasn't worried about being gentlemanly while I did it."

"Okay." April's acknowledgment was begrudging, even though she could see his point. The patterns ingrained in her from the marriage to Freeman could not be overcome so easily.

Asta whimpered; she was holding him too tightly. April made herself relax, repeating to herself that Tony was a better man than Freeman. He'd actually seemed to appreciate her own contribution to the melee at the Winner's Circle, useless though it had been. He'd even hinted that they were partners...maybe *equal* partners. Certainly Freeman would never have dreamed of such a thing.

April locked her gaze with Tony's, even though she was trembling inside. "I want you to understand my reaction, too, Tony. And that means I have to tell you about my marriage to Freeman Pierce." Not her favorite pastime, but it was overdue. She owed it to Tony if they were to be partners.

He did look so handsome, with his short black hair and his skin honey brown against a crisp white polo shirt, and so concerned, with his brown-black eyes meeting hers, rich with empathy. April felt as though her heart had been squeezed tight and was now beating too rapidly in distress. It was similar to—but totally different than—the stifling, choking sensation she'd experienced around Freeman. And the difference, she acknowledged warily, was too vast to be accounted as a merely physical attraction. Perhaps this wasn't going to be an easy-come, easy-go relationship after all. Perhaps they were going to be even more than partners.

She took a deep breath. "When we were newlyweds, I thought Freeman's lavish attentions were a symptom of his love. He said so, often. And I was charmed.

"I didn't fully recognize that his actions had become obsessive until I started counting the number of times I'd been out of his sight since the wedding. And the limited contact I'd had with my friends. He interfered, and he arranged things, insidiously at first, then openly. He pretended that he was giving me what I wanted, but the truth was that I was constantly capitulating to him. He wanted to control every detail of my existence. Even my thoughts, or so it seemed in the worst moments."

Tony grimaced. "So when I ordered you around at the Winner's Circle..."

April nodded. "Yes, I was reacting more to my experience with Freeman than to you."

"Free-man," he mused. "An ironic name."

"Don't I know it."

"I'm sorry, April."

She longed to collapse into his arms, but traces of mistrust and caution held her back. Her chin went up instead and she snapped, "I won't accept your pity. And I will not spend my life apologizing. The fact is that when Freeman was killed in the airplane accident, I'd already broken away. People were calling me a widow, but I felt more like reveling in my freedom."

"Which you're doing..." Tony said contemplatively.

"Don't tell anyone. The truth might spoil The Madcap Heiress's reputation for mindless frivolity."

He smiled a little. "Maybe it's time to give her up?"

Did he want her to? Did he think she was too outlandish for a conservative archaeology professor? April squirmed inside. If she wanted to be more than temporary partners with Tony Farentino, would she be forced to conform? And mightn't that be only the beginning of what he'd request—or demand—of her?

"The Madcap Heiress suits my purposes," she said, reverting to snootiness. Then qualified the statement. "For the moment."

Before Tony could reply, a sleek black art deco telephone chirped from the bedside table. April stretched out a languid hand to answer it. "Pierce residence."

"*Aaaye-pril,*" keened Dunky.

"Oh!" She bounced up onto her knees, caught Tony's eye and sank back down. Despite their tentative partnership, her instinctive reaction was to conceal Dunky's identity. "Oh...hello, there," she said more casually. Maybe after she knew for sure the fate of the Fogbottom she could include Tony. And maybe not.

"April, I didn't want to take your painting, but I had to. Talon said I had to if I wanted the money to pay my bookie. She said nobody would get hurt, but I didn't want to do it. I swear I didn't want to do it."

"I know. It's okay. Just tell me where you are and we'll figure something out." Tony was looking too interested; she had to distract him. "Just a sec," she said to Dunky and put her hand over the mouthpiece. She pointed to the one-armed reclining couch angled before the fireplace. "Tony, I forgot to return your vest from the other day. Remember? It's on the couch over there, and the retainer is still in the pocket. You really should keep better track of your money."

He got up, but he eyed the telephone suspiciously. "Is that—"

"Lady Eve. The silly thing is lost." She made shooing motions. Asta nipped at her marabou feathers. "Go on, get the vest. I'll be just a moment."

"JUST A MOMENT" later, Tony found himself back in his car at the curb in front of the town house, the engine idling, the suede vest folded neatly into the box resting in his lap. After a whispered conference on the phone, April had scooted out of bed and disappeared into her walk-in closet, nattering something about taking the afternoon off for a shopping spree with Lady Eve. Even though he'd wanted to discuss the case and what they'd each learned at the Winner's Circle, April had feigned uninterest and dismissed him in her haughty heiress voice without even coming back out to face him.

Having thought for a few fleeting moments that they'd reached some sort of simpatico, Tony was now suspicious, to say the least.

He lifted off the top of the box, parted a double layer of tissue paper and took out the vest. The envelope containing April's retainer was still in the pocket. How could he have forgotten about the money when it was what had initially led him into dabbling with this case?

Too large a dose of April Pierce had gone to his head, even making him crazy enough to imagine he was falling in love with her. Hell. If he lost all his acumen, who was going to give him a grant to reexcavate the tomb at Cayaxechun?

He lifted the vest and realized that there was something else in the pocket. Instantly thoughts of Cayaxechun were a million miles away as he scooped out a small, flat square object—the slide he'd picked off the floor of Donkey's sitting room. He held it up toward the sun and squinted.

It was a negative of a painting. There was a lot of water, a boat under full sail. A red-and-white striped beach umbrella in the sand. And a tiny little lady wading in the surf. A tiny little naked lady.

The Fogbottom?

Though April had never told him exactly what old Lesley Orville Fogbottom had painted that was worth so much money, she'd mentioned that he specialized in nudes. This could be *the* Fogbottom, but why would Donkey need a slide of it when he already had the actual painting? For that matter, why had he disappeared with the Fogbottom? Why not just turn it over to Talon and her "buyer with big bucks and an inflated sense of his own expertise"—or words to that effect?

"Slides," Tony whispered. That was it—the clue that had been on the tip of his tongue!

The young artist they'd met on the staircase at Talon's gallery had mentioned slides of her artwork. Subconsciously he'd realized there was a connection between this slide and the stolen Fogbottom. And April had successfully distracted him before he could put the two together.

The question was still *why?* What was Donkey doing with slides of the Fogbottom? Why had Talon, potentially his partner in the caper, resorted to hiring the thugs to look for her brother? Why had April hired a P.I. when there were times she seemed to prefer that Tony did not actually solve the crime?

Suddenly he knew. Tony hit the steering wheel with the flats of his hands. It was so obvious!

He slammed the gearshift into Drive and took a perverse pleasure in burning rubber on his way out of Palace Circle and onto Lake Shore Drive.

Tony Farentino, P.I. extraordinaire, was returning to Windenhall.

TWENTY EIGHT MILES NORTH of the Milwaukee bypass, April and her gleaming white convertible took an exit. Tony, following at a discreet but not necessarily surreptitious distance, did the same. Exactly twelve minutes later, the cavalcade arrived at Belle Terre, a small Wisconsin town whose main street was hilly and wide, festooned with the brilliant late spring green of twin rows of towering elms.

April turned into a small parking lot and went into a convenience store. Tony parked on the street, waited a minute, then got out to feed a coin into the meter. He sauntered toward the convenience store and peered in the window.

He was in time to see April disappear down an aisle, wheeling a shopping cart. Except for the fuzzy white mohair sweater draped around her shoulders, she was dressed all in lilac: a blouse with the tails tied above her belly button, short denim skirt, lace-trimmed anklets, canvas shoes. She looked awfully cute and sprightly for such a cunning dissembler.

Tony had been so optimistic after she'd told him about her bad marriage and how it had influenced her present life-style. It wasn't just that he was finally getting to know the inner woman; what he'd cherished most was her trust in him.

Hah. Turned out only one of them was trustworthy, and it wasn't April Marie-Therese Throckmorton Fairchild Pierce.

He deliberately hardened his heart. Right from the start, she'd been sending him on wild-goose chases. In retrospect, he should have first gotten suspicious when she'd shown up in Rocco's office with that terribly convenient envelope of money. Not even heiresses carried so much cash.

So she'd bought him. That was his fault as much as hers. But the question remained: Was this just another of The Madcap Heiress's escapades? Or a scheme more diabolical?

He growled something nasty under his breath. Whichever it was, he felt duped. And manipulated. Not unlike the way he'd felt when he'd returned from South America to learn Howard X. Devlin had used his daddy's millions to play politics with the tenure committee.

Tony entered the store and lingered at a cardboard display stand, thumbing through seed packets as he kept a lookout. April crossed an aisle, her cart loaded with a jug of soda and cheese popcorn in a cellophane bag the size of a pillow. Sidling along the aisle, he craned his neck to see over a top row of shampoo bottles. She was examining a rack of paperback books.

His trip to Windenhall had been swift and successful and he'd lucked onto April and her convertible as they passed him on the expressway, cruising in the opposite direction. He'd lost time getting turned around, but her progress had been easy to track. She'd driven straight north, across the Illinois state line, around 150 miles total. This was her first stop. Which put the lie to her Lady-Eve-shopping-trip excuse. He'd been right to be skeptical of her telephone call. Time would tell if the caller had actually been, as he suspected, her dear friend Donkey.

She put a couple of books into her cart. *Mallory's Oracle* and the latest John Sandford mystery, Tony noted, hardly even bothering to hide himself. If she turned, she might spot him, but he couldn't make himself care. What harm was a bit of spying when April had been lying to him all along?

She paused by the magazines, selecting a few at random, then adding a *TV Guide*. The wheels of her cart squealed as she pivoted it back toward Tony. He ambled into the next aisle and watched her choose soap, shampoo, deodorant, disposable razors.

His eyebrows slashed upward. Just a wild guess, he told himself, but didn't it look as though someone was, oh, what the heck, maybe... *hiding out?*

April lingered at a shelf stacked with boxes of condoms. Tony held his breath while she made a selection; it was a brand with the optimistic—or intimidating—name of *Legend.* Okay, so who were the condoms for? he wondered, clenching his jaw, still holding his breath. Donkey was just a friend, wasn't he? Tony's cheeks ballooned. Or was April on her way to an assignation with someone else? His face took on a bluish tint.

April, squeaking toward the checkout, missed Tony's sudden exhale, but a display of colorful pinwheels spun in the blast of hot air. After a moment, he regrouped and silently exited through the entrance door.

A long lottery banner advising the easy route to millionairehood shielded him from April's view as he skulked past the windowed facade. He'd have liked to hang around to see her expression when she realized he'd followed her, but decided he'd better hold off until she led him to Donkey. Otherwise, knowing April, she'd insist that this *was* her shopping spree and Lady Eve, in search of her milkmaid roots, had gotten so lost she'd wound up in a dairy barn in Wisconsin.

April didn't return to her car immediately. She crossed the street and went into a bakery. Tony couldn't resist spying on what vital item she'd purchase there. He put his nose to the window and cupped his hands around his eyes. Inside, April pointed at a tray of plump éclairs with silky dark chocolate frosting.

Tony's smile wasn't really a smile. *Gotcha,* he thought. Or, as The Madcap Heiress herself might've said: *Bingo.*

LOGIC AND CLARITY were not Dunky's strong suits. April had found his garbled directions to be of no use at all, so she'd asked at the bakery about the easiest route to Veronica Lake. The gravel road she'd been directed to twisted through Wisconsin's beautiful moraine country. Conifers intertwined overhead, forming a cool, leafy tunnel. Fragrant dark green balsam boughs brushed the car. April drove slowly, checking mailbox numbers.

Although Dunky had panicked and run when the thugs had made a threatening attempt to collect what he owed his bookie, he'd luckily chosen the last place anyone who knew him would think to look. To Dunky, Windenhall's manicured acres were as country as he wanted to get. In pleading for April's rescue, he'd declared all of Wisconsin a dangerous jungle.

A dented tin mailbox was almost hidden in a bramble of blackberry bushes. 218B. Dunky's hidey-hole. April turned her car onto the rutted driveway. A low-slung wood frame cottage with peeling white paint was just ▾visible through the trees, its seedy lawn sloping to the lake. In another week the trees and underbrush would be in full leaf and the house would probably be completely sheltered from the road. The parking area—a few square yards of bare ground—was empty. Dunky had explained that he'd taken a bus, then a taxi. He'd sold his snazzy little German-made roadster months ago to fund his gambling addiction.

Dunky burst from the cottage when April stepped out of her convertible. Arms open, he waddled toward her in tasseled evening slippers, silk slacks and a smoking jacket, his open mouth working in a soundless, joyful welcome. A flush of relief pinked his pudgy cheeks.

"Awk!" April blurted in shock. "What have you done to your hair?"

Dunky took her into his arms. "April, April, April," he burbled. "I am so glad to see you."

"You—your hair!" she sputtered, crushed to his comfortably padded torso. She wrenched away from his clinging arms, stepped back and stared. Dunky's normally dark brown hair was now a bright, carroty orange. As a disguise, it would work only in a crowd of clowns.

"It was the peroxide," he explained, fussing with the wavy forelock. "I bought two bottles in town to bleach my hair blond. I had in mind a lovely golden shade like Robert Redford's, but something must've gone wrong because this—" he pointed at his orange head "—is what I got."

April groaned. "You should've stuck to Clairol."

"Is that the brand you use?" Dunky simpered with a twinkle in his eyes.

"Well, I'm glad to see you've still got your pluck. Come and see what I've brought you." She started pulling packages from the car. "All your favorites," she said, showing him the junk food and the mysteries. "I thought we could drive into town later to stock up on groceries, but for now—" she opened the white bakery box with a flourish "—dessert!"

It was the first time chocolate éclairs didn't bring a smile to Dunky's face. "But I want to come back to Chicago!" he wailed. "I can't take any more of this uncivilized jungle. You should hear the racket—the birds, the ducks, that ever-lapping lake, the howling and hooting in the night and the continual rustling and crackling in the woods. I can't sleep a wink, thinking it's either the goons or a grizzly bear coming to get me!''

"I don't believe there are grizzlies in Wisconsin—"

"Whatever," he said, moping. "Can't I come back? Please? I'll check into the Drake Hotel under an assumed name." He swooned. "Oh, to have fresh sheets, a well-stocked bar and room service . . ."

"No, Dunky," April said firmly, and felt as if she'd just torn the wings off a butterfly when Dunky sagged in dejection. "You must stay out of sight until I've settled up with the thugs." *And Talon,* she thought, not saying it out loud because she wasn't sure how much Dunky knew. He might panic again if she let it slip that the thugs had apparently been hired by his own sister.

Dunky's expression turned hopeful. "Settle up?"

She sighed. "Yes, Dunky, I'll pay your gambling debt. I would have given you the money in the first place if I'd known you were desperate enough to steal my Fogbottom."

"I didn't steal it, April, honey." He tugged on his burgundy velvet lapels, lifting his square but weak chin out of his silk ascot. Darryl Dunkington had his own unique code of honor. "I only borrowed it."

She nodded. "That was what I figured. But you should have told me, Dunky. When you turned up missing, I thought the thugs had, um, gotten ahold of you."

"They said they would bust my kneecaps." He relayed this with a certain relish, now that he wasn't so alone and afraid. "But what really got to me was when they threatened to break all my fingers." He held out his hands so they could both admire them. "These puppies are worth more than a measly one hundred and fifty thousand!"

"Certainly," April said, trying to look stern. "If only you'd use them for good instead of evil."

"My faux masterpieces do no harm."

"Dunky, that's no longer true. I wish you could see that you're hurting yourself most of all." She took the bags from the convenience store and walked to the cottage. "I want you to promise me that there'll be no more questionable artwork after I pay your debt. We'll first find you some help for your gambling problem, and when you start painting again you'll stick to Darryl Dunkington originals. Won't you?"

Dunky opened a screen door patched with silver duct tape and stepped aside for April. Although he didn't look happy, he was in no position to argue. "I guess. Maybe..."

She kicked open the wooden inner door and stood firm on the threshold. "No maybe about it, Dunky. Promise me or you won't get the money." Ruthlessness took some practice, but it was the only way to deal with someone as weak-willed as Dunky.

He nudged past her, the bakery box cradled to his abdomen. "Oh, all right. I promise I'll go straight. Straight as a yardstick. Straight as a Boy Scout." He chuckled. "Straight as a poker hand."

"So we have a bargain." April knew she'd have to keep a close eye on him. "Now." She hefted the jug of soda pop. "Where's the fridge?"

"Ooh, you've got to see it—it's so retro!" Dunky enthused. He was bustling into the grimy, old-fashioned kitchen when there was a heavy knock at the door.

April and Dunky froze, staring at each other with round eyes. The unexpected and uninvited visitor rapped at the door, rattling the hinges.

"The goons!" Dunky hissed. "They followed you."

April looked at the door, which shook alarmingly under the continued hammering. "I—I don't think so," she whispered, but she couldn't be sure. They'd followed her before.

Dunky heard the worry in her voice. He jerked around in frantic circles, his arms pinwheeling helplessly as he searched for a hiding place. The cottage was basically just one room, with a dining ell and an open kitchen. Except for the bathroom, the prospects for concealment weren't good.

The hammering stopped for a few seconds, then started again louder than ever, startling Dunky into action. He raced across the room, losing a shoe, slipping on the rag rugs, and dived into the bed he'd made out of the foldout sofa. Its springs sang in distress. Dunky reached for the tangle of bedclothes. He yanked a fusty army blanket over his head.

For a moment April's reason deserted her. She scrambled over to the sleeper sofa and tried to fold it up—with Dunky inside. He squealed in protest. She threw all her weight into jamming the thin mattress and heavy frame into place.

"Glug," said Dunky in a muffled voice.

"Awk," croaked April, looking down. Dunky's denuded foot protruded from one end of the half-folded sofa, the fringe of his carrot top and an outflung arm from the other. When she released her wrestling hold and stepped back, the bottom two-thirds of the bed opened with a rattle and a clang.

April shook her head dumbly. This was crazy. Utterly ridiculous. What in the world did she think she was doing?

Another knock. This time someone was rapping at the glass sliding doors that opened onto a sagging cedar deck with a view of the lake. April turned slowly, fully expecting to see Eldridge peering inside, his beady little eyes gleaming with finger-breaking malice.

Dunky's head emerged from the blanket. "Who is *that?*" he quavered.

April did a double take.

It was Tony.

7

Love Me, Love Me Not

"Donkey forged the Fogbottom."

April's tiny gasp gave her away. Dunky drew himself up. "Absolutely not," he blustered. His fair complexion grew rosy with the lie.

"Oh, yeah?" Tony snapped. He paced the cottage in several long strides, looking for evidence. After they'd let him in, he'd sat April and her buddy on the edge of the sofa bed and told them to stay put; they still were, whispering to each other furiously. The mysterious Darryl Dunkington might have been handsome—if it weren't for the strangely orange hair—in a pampered, doughy, playboyish way. Although the condom purchase had renewed his curiosity about the nature of their relationship, seeing firsthand April's purely friendly concern for Donkey had at least set those doubts aside. Clearly they were just comrades. Comrades in crime.

"Turpentine," Tony said, snatching up a tin from beside the paint-stained kitchen sink. He waved it under their noses. "Painters clean their brushes with turpentine."

"Turpentine has many uses," Dunky insisted. "Why, I use it for—for—"

"Give it up, Dunks," April said out of the side of her mouth.

Meanwhile Tony had found a treasure trove of blatant evidence in a small closet. He started pulling out items. "An easel." It clattered to the floor. "A roll of canvas. Aha—brushes!" He'd sneaked into Windenhall to check on the state of Donkey's art supplies and had discovered that all of the paintbrushes and most of the oil paints were missing. Which had meant there was a good chance his hunch about the missing playboy being a forger was right on the money. "Charcoal drawings—" preliminary sketches of the Fogbottom fluttered across the floor like falling leaves "—and paints!"

April caught one of the tubes Tony was shoveling out of the closet. "Okay, okay, you've made your point."

He wasn't ready to quit. "A projector," he announced triumphantly, lifting it off the floor and setting it on a table. Eyes on April, he removed the incriminating slide from his pocket. He held it up for both of them to see, but continued watching only her. She didn't look as guilty or as remorseful as he thought she should.

"It was the slide that did it," he told her. "If you hadn't left it in my vest pocket with the envelope of cash, I might never have made the connection."

"I didn't even know it was there!"

"But you definitely knew you were manipulating me. I'll bet you never wanted a legitimate P.I. at all." Which didn't really jibe when you thought it through with a cool head, he admitted to himself. April would've had no idea who'd be at the desk when she'd donned her peacock feathers and fluttered into Farentino Investigations with her hefty retainer.

"I did!" she insisted, then averted her lavender eyes. "But, yes, I knew that Dunky wasn't going to sell the genuine Fogbottom to Talon. I tried to tell you—"

That was true, too. "But you didn't tell me *why*. A crucial omission, I'd say."

She shrugged. "I was afraid you'd insist Dunky be arrested. I had to find out where he'd gone with the painting, but I couldn't be responsible for sending him to prison."

"Prison!" Dunky squeaked, as though the possibility had never occurred to him. Given his world of privilege, perhaps it hadn't, Tony thought. Too much money had a way of cushioning a person from life's cruel realities. Look at April.

"Commit the crime, do the time," he said without pity.

"B-b-but, I n-never..." With his eyeballs rolling in their sockets, Dunky threw up his hands and collapsed flat against the unmade bed in a theatrical faint. April shot Tony a withering look before bending over her friend. She murmured soothingly and fanned him with the fringed end of his satin sash.

Not in the mood for such mollycoddling, even if he'd begun to understand the motive behind April's deception, Tony turned back to the closet. Behind a folded lawn chair he found two canvases shrouded in sheets. Conscious of the Fogbottom's worth, he lifted them out carefully. April revived Dunky in time for the unveiling.

Tony unwrapped the first painting. Framed in heavy gilt scrollwork, it was a seascape of muted pastels and glowing whites. Waves swelled, gulls soared, the sailboat bobbed. The wading nude figure was L. O. Fogbottom's version of Venus on the half shell.

"My Fogbottom." April sighed, her face smoothing out as she gazed at the tranquil scene. She hugged Dunky. "Thank you for keeping it safe from the thugs."

He beamed. "It was a big sacrifice, spending a week in the wilderness, but somebody had to do it."

"Excuse me?" In Tony's estimation, Donkey looked altogether too pleased with himself and all the trouble he'd caused. And April seemed to have forgotten the situation—she was rewarding the outlaw with hugs! "Excuse me, but the Fogbottom wouldn't have been endangered if Donkey hadn't stolen—"

"Borrowed!" Dunky sang.

"—*borrowed* it in the first place."

"Oh, you're just cranky because I didn't let you in on the entire story right from the beginning," April said with a cavalier toss of her head. "It wasn't *my* fault you assumed Talon wanted to sell a stolen Fogbottom instead of a forged one, but I'll apologize anyway for the minuscule role I had in the mix-up." She slung her arm around Dunky's shoulders. "Besides, all's well that ends well, no?"

"No," Tony said blackly. "Not yet." Dramatically he swept the covering off the second painting.

To the naked eye it appeared to be an almost exact copy of the Fogbottom, the only major differences being its newer, fresher look and the lack of a frame. "Easy," Dunky cautioned as Tony set the forgery next to the original. "The paint is still wet."

"Dunky," breathed April. Her gaze slid back and forth, comparing the two paintings. "It's an astonishing likeness!"

He preened. "Isn't it, just?"

"Just," Tony repeated, heavy on the sarcasm. "Just about ten to fifteen in the slammer." Dunky turned bilious.

"Fortunately," April stressed, "we've stopped you in time. Talon will never receive this painting, meaning it won't be sold as an original to Nelson McNair, and thus no crime has been committed. Is that clear, Dunky?" She tightened her grip on him.

"The goons," he groaned.

"Tony and I will take care of them."

"We will?" Tony asked. "Wasn't one encounter with them enough for you?"

"Somebody has to pay them off, and I'm afraid I've volunteered. T-Bone isn't such a terrible guy—just a little misguided." With a mournful sigh, April turned the full force of her limpid eyes on Tony. Her heart-shaped face was as open and guileless as a babe's. He didn't believe it for a second. "But that's okay, Tony. You don't have to accompany me. I'll handle the entire transaction myself."

With a growl he jammed his fists into the pockets of the black vest. "Like hell you will."

She popped off the bed. "I knew you'd forgive me, darling Tony," she trilled and gave him a quick kiss on the cheek. "Don't worry, it'll be a snap. The thugs will be so thrilled to see all that cash, they wouldn't dream of hurting either one of us."

"Has it occurred to you that paying Donkey's gambling debt only takes care of the bookie's threats? What about Talon—wasn't she the one who hired the thugs in the first place?"

"Not Talon!" Dunky said.

April shook her head sorrowfully. "I'm afraid so."

"But when they first recognized me at the jailhouse, it was because my bookie already had them looking for me," Dunky explained. "They tracked me to Windenhall and told me to pay up fast, or else."

"Maybe that was where Talon met them, then," April said excitedly. "And when you disappeared with the Fogbottom and she didn't hear from you or receive the forgery, she hired the thugs to find you again."

"Which brings us back to my point," Tony said. "Talon will not be pleased that April's paying the debt, since that means she won't have a forgery to pass off to McNair."

Dunky shrugged. "MacArthur will bail the gallery out. He always does."

"All we have to do is get the cash at my bank and arrange a meeting with the thugs," April said with relish. "Then Dunky'll be in the clear."

Dunky looked up from stuffing his foot back into his tasseled black leather evening slipper. "You know," he ventured hopefully, "it'd be a shame to see all that lovely cash go straight to the goons. I could replenish your account, April, if you're willing to risk the payoff money. I know a place where I can double the sum in twenty minutes."

April shrieked with sheer exasperation and tossed the army blanket back over his gaudy orange head.

THE LATE-AFTERNOON sun dappled Veronica Lake, penetrating the shallows with shafts of sunlight that illuminated the pebbly bottom. A breeze blew in gentle puffs across the water, rippling the surface, wavering the green strands of waterweeds, fingering through April's blond hair. She adjusted her wide white mohair headband.

"Dunky was doing it long before I met him," she said to Tony as they strolled along the narrow strip of sand that ringed most of the lake. "It started when one of the Dunkington family portraits was damaged during a wild weekend house party. While his parents were out of town, Dunky painted a substitute and replaced the original, with no one except the butler the wiser. Then a friend with a cash flow problem asked him to paint a few look-alikes to impress the girls he invited up to his penthouse pied-à-terre. After that, a little word of mouth and, presto, Dunky was producing a steady stream of what he prefers to call 'masterpiece replicas.'"

"They're still forgeries." Tony clenched his hands inside the pockets of his khaki shorts. "And it's still a shady business, no matter what he calls it."

"Not really. The replicas aren't priced as originals because they're not meant to be forgeries." April paused to watch a school of minnows flicker through the aquamarine water. "Dunky may copy the original artist's signature on the front, but he signs his own on the back. Until the Fogbottom, he hadn't meant to truly fool anyone, except perhaps those who never look beyond the surface."

"According to Rocco, prisons are chock-full of criminals swearing their intentions were good."

April's mouth set stubbornly. "Be that as it may. I know Dunky and he was only—"

"Planning to cheat an art collector out of a quarter of a million dollars, according to big sis Talon."

"The thugs were threatening to break his fingers!"

"He could've gone to the police."

She shook her head. "His father would never have forgiven him for besmirching the family name with such publicity."

"Gambling and carousing with the Palace Circle Pranksters doesn't qualify?"

"I didn't say that." She frowned. Tony was probably stating his own opinion, and not all that subtly, either. He surely meant to include *her,* the leader of the Pranksters, among the besmirchers. "You don't understand."

He was staring across the lake at the summer cottages and cabins crowding the shoreline. Since it was early in the season yet, most of them appeared empty. "I understand that Donkey and Talon feel they're above the law." His voice was hard. "Remember, I've seen the damage done to a country's historic heritage when wealthy collectors consider themselves to be above the law. They purchase art and antiquities from the smugglers who've pillaged archaeological sites. It's not just a shady occupation—it's sleazy, slimy and utterly beneath contempt."

She felt chilled despite the warm sun. "I never said I condoned Dunky's plan," she protested. "After all, I hired you so we could stop him before he went through with the scheme.''

Tony swiped his hand over his face, then regarded April with apology. ''No, you're not to blame. You were trying to help, even though you went about it in a rather convoluted way.''

She bit her lip. ''I know that Dunky is irresponsible and spoiled.'' She supposed that she often came across the same way. After viewing herself through Tony's eyes, such a likelihood didn't please her. Maybe it *was* time to abandon The Madcap Heiress persona...

But back to Dunky. ''And giving him the money to pay his gambling debt means he's let off the hook again,'' she continued, before Tony could. ''I've always suspected he'd rather produce legitimate work, anyway. Perhaps this time he'll finally go straight.'' Perhaps this time she'd make certain that he did.

Tony ran his palm along the outside of her arm. If she'd been a cat her fur would have stood on end, crackling with electricity. ''You're a better friend than he deserves,'' he said.

The corners of her lips twitched up. ''Well, I've been looking for a way to get rid of the last of the settlement money. I guess this is it.''

He took her hand. ''What settlement money?''

Yikes. She'd forgotten she hadn't told him about that. ''It's nothing,'' she mumbled. In some ways, that was true. Symbolically and monetarily, however, the settlement loomed large. ''Only a, um, certain sum that I was awarded in compensation for Freeman's accidental death.'' She wrinkled her nose. ''It feels wrong, putting it that way. I didn't particularly want the money.''

Tony's eyes were bright with curiosity. ''So you're— what did you say? Getting *rid* of it?''

She nodded. ''If I did it Freeman's way, the money would be locked up in long-term certificates of deposit or stodgy government bonds. I'd have to think about it for the rest of my life. My way, I spend it as quickly as possible."

"Interesting," Tony murmured. The breeze ruffled his hair, the sunshine glancing off the blue-black highlights.

April's heart brimmed with unexpected emotion. "Freeman may have wangled a way to control my Throckmorton trust fund even from beyond the grave, but he didn't foresee dying so suddenly. He also overlooked his own insurance. And that I was still the beneficiary." She blinked her watering eyes several times, her voice reverberating with shaky defiance. "I guess blowing the last of the money on getting Dunky out of his jam is one way of proving I'm beyond Freeman's control, but..."

"But?" Tony prompted with a squeeze of his hand.

April slipped her hand free, then laced her fingers through his instead. She didn't want to be enfolded and protected. She preferred an equal connection... an intertwining partnership.

"I had considered giving the remainder of the money to you, Tony. To fund your dig in Guatemala." She felt rather bashful about broaching the offer, even if it was no longer possible. She wasn't sure that he'd be interested. He certainly hadn't leaped at her mention of endowing a chair at his college. Maybe he was one of those men who thought it beneath him to accept money from a woman for any reason—an attitude she considered not only overly prideful but insulting and condescending, too.

"Generous, as always," he murmured, sliding his other hand around her waist and drawing her over so she faced him. "But I'm not interested. I don't want your money, April."

"Oh." She closed her eyes and swallowed the lump rising in her throat. "Of course not. I shouldn't have even brought it up. It was just a silly impulse—"

"I'd rather have your heart."

She rocked backward. Tony caught her, both hands on her waist, holding her tight enough so she stayed upright as his words seemed to hover in the sunlit air. She squinted through her eyelashes at the gilding of Tony's sculpted features and shadowing of the hollows beneath his cheekbones and the dent of his dimple. A hitch developed in her chest—when she opened her mouth all that came out was a soft, raspy *awk*.

She summoned some of her heiress-style composure and tried again. "You'd rather...? I thought you were angry with me."

"I was steaming. When I figured out what Donkey was up to with the Fogbottom, it seemed as though you'd been playing games with me, for whatever reason, right from the start. But now I see that it was just a misguided attempt to protect Donkey." He narrowed his eyes. "Not that he deserved it. And not that you shouldn't have told me right away when he called this morning, instead of misleading me and taking off by yourself. What if the thugs had followed you and not just me?" His fingers splayed over her hips. "It would have been nice if you'd trusted me at least that much."

As April's insides flowed with warmth, every emotion she'd stored in her heart this past week yearned toward him. The pull was so strong she was amazed to realize that she still stood in place. "I do—I do trust you," she whispered brokenly.

He lifted one hand to her hair and gently played his fingers through the buttercup-colored wisps and waves floating free of the fuzzy headband. "Then you have a fine way of showing it."

She closed her eyes again, letting the smooth bass of his voice resonate through her. "Dunky didn't want—" she started to say, then stopped herself. She couldn't blame her shortcomings on Dunky. Not even on Freeman, forever. Either Tony deserved her trust or he didn't. Either she could give it or she couldn't.

April looked at him, so sure and strong and male against the backdrop of the blue-green lake and the dark fringe of the forest. *He did.* He deserved everything good she could offer. But...*could* she? Was it possible to learn to love again?

Her lips parted softly. "How can I convince you?"

"Like this," he murmured. His hand tightened in her hair, cupping the base of her skull as his head lowered to hers. The yearning surged through her again and this time she rose with it to greet his lips. Tony held her close as they kissed. She burrowed against him, feeling his chest heave with uneven breaths, feeling his lips hesitate momentarily, then touch hers so gently she knew he was holding himself in check. Perhaps he'd sensed her doubt and was afraid of grabbing and crushing what was such a fragile beginning of trust.

"Like this," she murmured throatily, deepening the kiss with a long, slow, satiny glide of her lips and tongue.

"Like *this*," he said with a rumbling chuckle. His mouth was open, his tongue sweetly invasive as it stroked against hers. April's yearning turned to an ache, a hard knot of wanting lodged deep in her belly.

Tony released her. "It's either stop now or keep kissing until only a plunge in the lake will cool us off."

"Hmm," she hummed, as if weighing the alternatives. "Which do you prefer?"

He glanced toward the cottage. "Donkey can take care of himself for a few more days. Why don't we get back to the city?"

"If that's what you want."

His coffee-colored eyes were hot with desire. "What I want won't wait much longer than one hundred and fifty miles, a good hot meal and a comfortable bed. A private bed."

Ah—finally he was willing to forgo their business relationship for a more personal encounter! April teased him with a smoldering look of half-lowered lashes and pouty lips. "No sleazy motels and assumed names?" she asked playfully. "I've always wanted to check in as *Mildred Pierce*."

"Not this time. I want everything to be perfect."

"Goodness," she breathed in admiration. "That's a tall order." Her gaze traveled up the thickly muscled length of him. "But then, so are you."

Laughing, hands linked, they returned to the cottage to tell Dunky they were departing. When he started getting nervous about being left alone in the wilderness, Tony offered his car for the duration. Hoping Dunky was still too intimidated by the thugs to dare an outing to one of his various gambling venues, April lectured him strongly, having no compunction about holding the potential withdrawal of her payoff money over his head. Dunky flared briefly with indignation, then offered them his jug of root beer and peanut butter and jelly sandwiches for the road; he'd already consumed the éclairs. April suggested they take the Fogbottom instead, but Tony thought it would be safer at the Veronica Lake hideout for now. Orange hair flaming in the sunshine, Dunky disconsolately waved them out of the driveway.

Tony wanted to drive the convertible, so April let him, secretly smiling at the predictable male impulse to take command of all available machinery. But the smile faded away as they traveled down the gravel road in the watery green light that filtered through the trees. Wasn't it also a question of control? She worried. Once she and Tony had achieved a mutual accord, he'd instantly wanted to take charge. Suppose a precedent had already been set by her unthinking acquiescence . . .

Then again, it was only a car, she reflected, watching Tony's bare, brown, sinewy legs. A muscle flexed in his calf when he tapped the brake pedal. And Tony Farentino was nothing like Freeman Pierce. There was really no good reason for her to be a stickler on every minor point that came up.

April slid her sunglasses in place and relaxed back in the red leather seat. Fringed shadows cast by the tall evergreens crisscrossed her upturned face. *Everything is okay,* she told herself. *Everything is perfect.*

When they crossed the state line many miles later, she'd almost convinced herself.

ALTHOUGH DUSK comes late even in the earliest days of a Midwest summer, by the time they pulled into the driveway of Tony's small house in Wicker Park it had already arrived. April's empty stomach had been growling since the suburbs and Tony had promised her an impressive but quick home-cooked dinner.

The dim light revealed the clean lines of a Prairie-style tan brick house with white-and-black trim around its many windows. The hedges bordering the flagged walkway were in desperate need of barbering, but the small patch of lawn had been freshly mowed. Tony had admitted that he was rarely in residence during the summer break—he was usually participating in a dig halfway across the world—and that his house was more of a way station than a proper home.

April was pleasantly surprised by the interior. Although the white walls and lack of ornamentation seemed stark, there were also warm wooden floors scattered with nubby black-and-autumn-colored rugs, an elegantly simple Shaker dining table and chairs and a plump sandcolored couch long enough for Tony to stretch out on.

He brought her a glass of wine and disappeared back into the kitchen. She wandered around, touching the very few artifacts—an African mask, a few pottery fragments and an old coin—tucked among the rows of full book-

shelves covering an entire wall. She found a tiled bathroom and freshened up. She lowered herself into the
canvas sling of a butterfly chair placed before the windows. She sipped her wine and wondered if she'd been
wise to agree to a rendezvous on unfamiliar territory. Had
she reason to be wary?

Then she thought about Tony's eyes, his dimples, his
lips, his gorgeously tanned physique. About his sly humor, his intellect and occasional self-mocking denigra-
tion. His courage and daring, his fiery morality, his quick
forgiveness.

And she decided yes. *Yes* to everything, except the one
thing that Tony hadn't mentioned, the one thing that she
was afraid to believe in ever again.

APRIL CAME INTO the kitchen as Tony was sliding a pan
of six slices of stuffed sweet peppers—two each red, green
and yellow—under the broiler. Her nose twitched. "Now,
really, how did you accomplish that so fast?" she accused.

"I cheated," he admitted. "The stuffed peppers were
in the fridge, made yesterday."

"You cook like that just for yourself?"

"Once in a while. When I'm home." He set three garlic cloves on the butcher block and picked up a large chef's
knife. "You'll understand if you ever taste the terrible
camp stove food we eat at digs. This is makeup." *Bam*—
he slammed the heel of his hand down on the flat of the
knife and smashed the garlic.

April leaned her elbows on the counter. "I don't know
anything about cooking," she said cheerfully. "Grandmother Throckmorton and my mother conspired to keep
Gussy and me out of the kitchen. They were afraid we
would get up to mischief and annoy their temperamental
French chef." She reflected. "We did anyway—that was

probably why the chef was so temperamental—so they may as well have let him teach us to cook.''

While the garlic cloves sizzled in oil, Tony quickly chopped tomatoes and scallions. ''You have a brother?'' he asked, adding them to the skillet.

''No, Gussy is my younger sister. Augustina Isobel Throckmorton Fairchild.''

''Compared to you, she's a little light in the name department,'' he teased, wondering suddenly if April would ever consider shortening her own string to a simple April Farentino. He added capers to the skillet and stirred. Okay, so maybe he was jumping the gun again. Big-time. Although April wasn't quite the flibbertigibbet she was cracked up to be, he still couldn't imagine her settling down—except in his bed, and likely only briefly even there.

How could he get her to stay longer? Having a handle on her might help. ''Tell me more about your family,'' he urged.

''Our parents were always popping in and out, so Gussy and I lived with our grandparents. They were the old-fashioned, keep-a-stiff-upper-lip-while-you-take-your-cod-liver-oil types, but the family was really ruled by Great-grandfather Throckmorton. He's still alive, ninety-six and bedridden, but back then I thought he was a fire-breathing dragon.''

''Ah. So your late husband wasn't the first control freak in your life.''

April paled. ''No, I guess not...'' She attempted a wan smile. ''You can see why I finally had to break free. And why I might have gone a bit overboard.''

''Good for you. You deserved it.'' He meant that, too, but perhaps now a distraction was in order. He asked her to open a can of tuna while he took the broiled peppers from the oven. After tossing a half pound of linguine with the fish, cilantro and grated lemon peel, he distributed the portions on plates and they carried them out to the dining table. Abandoning her introspection, April eyed the meal hungrily while he went back for the wine.

She dipped a hunk of crusty bread into the olive oil he'd provided, then forked up a heaping bite of pasta. "Delicious, but all that garlic," she said, raising her eyebrows at him across the table.

Grinning, he passed her the platter of colorful goat-cheese-stuffed peppers. "You know what they say about garlic. Its effect is canceled out as long as we both partake."

Her lashes fluttered. "Then, by all means, eat up, darling Tony."

They both did, voraciously. Between bites she asked if he'd been taught to cook by his mother.

"Both my parents, really. My father is of Italian heritage, my mother Greek, so they compete in a no-holds-barred ethnic culinary competition. Every special occasion features a combined Mediterranean family feast. And I still get FedEx care packages. If you have a sweet tooth, there's phyllo dough for a dessert pastry in the freezer, courtesy of Mom." With a sneaky grin he added casually, "You can see why my four sisters weigh a collective half ton."

"What?" April said, mouth agape. "You're teasing me."

He couldn't contain his laugh. "Mom's *zaftig* and Pop swears his extra pounds are muscle, but my sisters' curves are all nicely proportioned. Actually they'd murder me if they knew I made a joke about their weight, even though they're always babbling about the newest diet."

"But of course." April nodded as if his prospective death sentence made perfect sense to her. It had to be a female thing, he decided, like the appeal of Fabio, headbands for bald babies and fifty-dollar jars of skin cream made with sheep placenta.

"So...perhaps you prefer a Marilyn Monroe figure on a woman? Maybe I should have that dessert."

He wondered if there was a blond bombshell wig and dress tucked inside her closet. He wouldn't be opposed, but... "How much I like the outside of a woman depends largely on how much I like the inside."

The slight trembling of her fingers on the fork betrayed her even as she scoffed, "Good answer, Tony. Very PC. Now can we try for the truth?"

He wasn't distracted. "All I know for certain is that I like you, April. Very much." He was mildly surprised to realize that he'd spoken the absolute truth, especially after this morning when he'd branded her a thoughtless conniver. Discovering that her previous life hadn't been as easy as one might assume of an heiress and that there were good reasons behind her present life-style had apparently made him change his mind again. This time around he was sure that the real April Pierce was not as capricious as April Peacock; she was often thoughtful, generous to a fault and, underneath the facade, extremely warmhearted. She was a curious mixture of innocence and sophistication, pure instinctive emotion and tightly held reserve.

"You're as beautiful inside as you are out," he concluded softly.

April didn't seem to know how to take the compliment. After a startled moment she smiled shyly, whispered a quiet "Thanks" and returned her attention to the food. Still, when Tony caught a glimpse of her eyes when he passed the breadbasket, he saw that they were luminous with unspoken pleasure.

Eventually they finished and brought the dishes back into the kitchen. They scraped, rinsed and loaded the dishwasher. April picked up a sponge and wiped down the counters and the stove top. She turned to see Tony watching her, one corner of his mouth lifted in amusement.

"I'm not completely undomestic," she explained. "I was once a waitress for several *very* long months." She saw no need to get into the circumstances behind that job, though she did feel compelled to add truthfully, "Not a very good one, however."

"You probably just wanted to acquire the uniform."

"It was ghastly! Pink A-line Dacron. With thick-soled white orthopedic shoes. I liked the little white apron, though."

"Mmm," he murmured, like a man contemplating a tasty dessert. "I'd like to see you in it..."

She wrinkled her nose. "Not on a bet." Tony was leaning against the counter in a sexy slouch, his head cocked as his gaze ran up from her shoes, lingered on the wedge of bare skin at her midriff, and finished at her face. The allure of the saucy French maid was one of those mystifying male things she didn't get, like kick-boxing, calling it "scoring" and paying extra for picture-in-picture so they could watch two boring baseball games at once.

"Not even in your wildest dreams," she taunted, then laughed and scrambled out of the kitchen when he came after her, a certain heated look in his eye.

Decorously April sat on the edge of the couch. Tony tuned a radio to a jazz station and sat beside her. A moment later, he was sprawled back into the corner and she was comfortably cuddled in the circle of his arms. Loving the contrast of warm male skin and crisp curling hairs, she slid her palm along his thigh below the edge of his shorts.

"Tell me why you became an archaeologist," she said, resting her chin in the hollow of his shoulder.

"That was also my parents' fault." With one finger he traced patterns between her shoulder blades, drawing curling lines of heat that wreaked havoc with her concentration. "They read us kids tales of mythology and ancient history as bedtime stories. The Greeks, Incas and Egyptians intrigued me, so I developed the interest throughout high school. Pop's a fisherman, with his own boat. He was disappointed that I didn't want to be his partner, but extremely proud when I got my Ph.D. and went into archaeology."

"What will you do now that you weren't granted tenure?"

His chest heaved with a sigh, but it was one of thought, not dejection. "I could find a position at another school, but to be honest, my heart was never in teaching anyway. I'd rather be doing fieldwork. So would about a hundred thousand other archaeologists. Competition for grants is fierce and the volume of paperwork's horrendous."

April thought she might have a way to solve that problem, but now was not the time. "Maybe you'll stay on at Farentino Investigations?" she suggested.

"Rocco's hoping I do, but Miss Estelle isn't, and I think we both know who runs that office. Besides, I'm not cut out for permanent gumshoeing."

"Hmm."

"Even though I did damn fine work on the Fogbottom case, if I do say so myself."

"Don't forget me," she reminded him with a nudge. "I helped immensely."

"Lola was more of a hindrance, though."

"Don't you dare insult Lola. Lola has a rapport with T-Bone. She could be a big help when we make the payoff."

Tony's body went as tight as a guitar string. She could have twanged the cords in the arm and wrist he'd draped across her stomach. "April..." he warned in an iron-fist-in-velvet-glove tone.

She lifted herself up a little and looked at him from the corner of her eye. "Tony, I will not take orders from you."

"The thugs are—"

"Dangerous. I know, I know. They're also more likely to go after you than me. Why should I have to stay home, waiting and worrying? Why can't we be equal partners?"

Exasperated, he let his head fall back against the arm of the couch. "You have no conception of how a man feels when his woman is in danger. I cannot let you—"

April flipped herself around and landed atop Tony with a soft thud. "Am I your woman?" she asked. "I hope so, because I've decided you're *my* man." She twined her arms around his shoulders and pushed her nose up against his, her pink lips stretching into a wide and blissful smile. "I'll never let anything bad happen to you, I promise."

Tony clutched his hair. "Lord, save me from this woman."

"Too late," she whispered, nipping at his square chin and its adorable indentation. "You may as well surrender, 'cause nothing can save you now."

"If that's the case..." He put his arms around her, one hand slipping low enough to cup her bottom. "I guess I'll go down with the ship."

"Oooh, naughty." She giggled, making darting forays with her tongue as she kissed a path along his jaw.

Tony turned his head and found her lips, seizing them as if he were a starving man. In one sense, he decided, he was. But he'd never have believed a week ago that the flighty peacock who'd walked into Rocco's office would turn out to be a full-course meal. And the very one he'd been craving, at that.

His tongue plunged past her lips with a bold stroke. April whimpered a little, but the movement of her hips and the twist of her fingers through his hair was surely an invitation for more. He brought his hands up to span her waist, his legs opening just enough so she was cradled between his thighs. He squeezed them a little tighter around her slim hips. The intimate contact was more than provocative; it was incendiary.

"...something I've been wanting to do," he mumbled, hungrily biting kisses from her lips, her cheeks, the arc of her neck. He slid one hand under her, found the knotted tails of her blouse and untied it with an impatient jerk. "Mmm, good."

His agile fingers played a riff up the front; the buttons neatly popped free of the buttonholes. "Even better," he said as the blouse parted to reveal a flimsy, lacy frill of a bra. A flick of his thumb and the clasp sprang open, baring April's breasts. They rested small but plump against the broad wall of his chest. "Best," he purred.

April braced her arms on either side of his shoulders and returned his kisses with an inexperienced but enthusiastic ardor, her hair falling forward, the curled ends tickling Tony's face as their lips fused, their tongues swirled. His muscled torso supported her perfectly; his thighs were hard, his arousal infinitely inspiring. A small doubt flashed through her, then dissolved in the warm rush of a passion so intense she had to pause to catch her breath.

Tony lifted her higher, moaning thickly when her thigh rubbed hard against him, provoking a deep, throbbing need. He thrust his face forward to reach her breasts. April sucked in another quick breath when the tip of his tongue and the pad of his thumb found her nipples, lapping and flicking them until they'd tightened even further, into small pink buds of acute sensation. He loved that he could give her such pleasure; his own blood ran hot in response.

"April, beautiful girl," he murmured, panting. She smelled like wind and water and sun-warmed lavender, but it almost hurt to draw breath. "I love you."

Although her reaction was instantaneous, it wasn't the one he'd expected. She stiffened, not with desire, but with—what? He wasn't sure. Was it...repulsion? Certainly rejection. Definitely denial.

April pushed away from him, her hands suddenly cold and stiff against his chest. Sitting on the very edge of the sofa, she pulled herself close and tight and stared at nothing, mesmerized, her eyes blank.

"What's wrong?" Tony blurted, his senses shocked out of the mood of steeping sensuality even if physically he still ached to continue.

She muttered something that sounded like "...you don't love me," and buried her face in her hands.

He sat up, reached for her, changed his mind and put only one hand out instead, gently laying it on the curve of her hunched back. She shuddered beneath his touch and slid away, walking swiftly to the window where she stood, gulping air, half sobbing, pulling her unbuttoned shirt tight and wrapping her arms around herself.

"But I do love you," he pleaded, misunderstanding.

"No." Her face was still averted, but he could tell by the strain in her voice that she was barely managing to force the words out. "*Don't*, I said. Don't love me. I don't want you to love me."

"April..." he murmured, wondering and hurting—for himself, but most of all for her. "Why?"

"Don't ask me that."

"I—" Tony rose, searching for the words that would reach her. She had seemed so eager but now she was freezing him out. What kind of craziness was this? "Don't you see? I have to ask, I have to know, because—"

April turned, an expression of controlled hauteur on her face. "Because?" she asked, her tone so clipped he would've known by that alone that this was not another case of playacting—even if there had been any doubt.

His answer was quiet but strong. "I can't stop loving you just because you tell me not to."

Her lips thinned. "Then I can't stay."

"And you won't tell me why."

A tear glinted softly in her eye. She swept it away with the back of her hand and drew herself up, totally in control. "It's simple, really, *dahling* Tony."

She was so cold the glitter of her eyes looked like light refracting on ice. "Madcap Heiresses are far too frivolous to believe in love," she said, and turned her back on him with an air of utter finality.

8

The Madcap Heiress Strikes Again

TONY HAD SURPRISED HER with the words *I love you,* but they were words April had heard before. Often.

I love you had been Freeman's catch phrase for every occasion. He'd used it first to romance her as a naive twenty-year-old, then to please her, and soon to placate her growing frustrations. He'd tossed it at her to stop her increasing inquiries, whispered it in velvety tones again and again as though it were the magic charm that would ignite her interest once their marriage had reached the point where she could no longer respond readily to his physical needs. He'd employed it to lure her back to San Francisco after she'd run away the first time. He'd tried it the second time, too, but by then she'd stopped believing those three deadly little words.

"Because I love you, April, honey. I love you." It had become Freeman's response to every confinement, postponement and commandment over which she'd railed. He'd used it so regularly and ultimately with so little meaning that his sudden death had indeed come as a relief, even though at that point they were separated and she usually only heard the words in her nightmares. At the funeral, April had prayed never to hear the phrase again.

Never? she asked herself now. Not even from Tony?

"Tony." April fell back into the plush support of the pillows heaped on her bed. What was she going to do about *him?*

"Poor Tony," she murmured, drawing an overstuffed gold brocade cushion to her abdomen and curling her legs and arms around it. It hadn't been his fault she'd instantly frozen up like a Popsicle at his unexpected recitation of the dreaded phrase. Poor, poor Tony had stared at her in shock as she'd responded to his entreaty with a cold shoulder and even colder words. Although eventually there'd been a touch of anger when she'd insisted on calling a cab, she'd sensed he'd been feeling mostly hurt, concern and bewilderment.

If only she'd maintained that frosty cool. Impatiently April turned her face away from the muffling cushion. Then she wouldn't have to feel so tortured now.

Oh, she'd tried, but by the next morning she'd thawed into mere numbness. At Lady Eve's discreet prodding, emotions had begun creeping in by that afternoon. Over dinner, the story had finally poured out of April in a flood of self-recrimination, though she'd stayed as dry-eyed as ever. Its telling had offered only a brief respite from the remorse eating at her. How could she have treated Tony so terribly when she knew very well that he was *not* Freeman Pierce?

"Bloody survival instinct," Lady Eve had said.

Now two days had passed without a word between them. April snuffled. Who could blame Tony for staying away?

She hissed a harsh word at herself and burrowed deeper into the pillows. Although Tony had responded obediently when she'd had Godfrey summon him to her bedside after their last spat, April didn't think such a high-handed approach would work this time. She was going to have to make the first move—even if it was just to arrange a business meeting that would draw the case and their acquaintance to a polite close.

God, but she didn't want that. An actual physical pain arrowed through April's curled body at the thought of losing Tony, leaving what felt like a hollow shaft right up through the aching heart of her. She moaned and clutched the pillows.

Fantasy had always come in handy at times like these. But she'd outgrown the poor little rich girl she'd been before her marriage to Freeman. And with the last of the insurance money pledged to Dunky, there was no more need to play the merry widow. The Madcap Heiress had served her purpose.

Or had she?

April sat up. What if there was a little life left in the old girl yet? What if The Madcap Heiress staged a comeback?

She liked that idea. After all, madcap heiresses didn't have doubts, or pain, or emotional baggage. They tossed their heads and laughed at the world. They twined men around their little fingers and collected so many hearts that every day was like Valentine's Day.

They definitely did not worry about three-word phrases that too many people flung to the wind like so much confetti. No, madcap heiresses plotted grand seductions, instead. They dated marvelous men and had fabulous affairs. And Tony responded to The Madcap Heiress in spite of himself.

"Eve," April called, pillows tumbling as she scrambled out of bed before her conscience could trick her into having second thoughts. "Eve, I've had such an idea! But I'll need your help. What do you remember of Miss Fibbing-White's calligraphy class?"

"Pardon?" her houseguest called back. "Did you say cartography?"

Gabbling happily about pen nibs, vellum and a menu for Godfrey, April slipped into a flowing silk kimono and glided down the gallery to the guest room where Lady Eve was packing for her return trip to London. Asta, curled into a ball of golden fur, lifted his head lazily and let out one halfhearted yip. Godfrey lurked near the closet with a steam iron, a shoe tree and the moony expression of a butler in love.

"Ah, you've risen from your couch of regret," said Lady Eve, folding a cashmere sweater. Godfrey rushed over with tissue paper. "Had enough wailing and breast-beating for today?"

April plopped onto the bed and arranged the voluminous silk around her bare legs. "I've thought of a way to lure Tony back to Palace Circle."

Lady Eve looked doubtful. "There's only one way, as I see it."

"Yes. I'm going to take the plunge," April said, thinking physical while her friend was referring to the opposite.

"Oh?" Lady Eve packed a lot of meaning into that one arch word. Godfrey, scowling, tucked another sheet of tissue into the suitcase.

"Madcap heiresses have tons of lovers. Scads of them. I've been derelict in my duty, so why not start with Tony?"

"*Start* with Tony?"

April tightened the sash of her robe, slightly irritated with Lady Eve's habit of asking questions so pithy and pointed she was forced to confront herself. "Why not?" she repeated, not as blithe as she might sound.

"Start *what* with Tony?"

April shot a glance at Godfrey and waited until he turned back to the ironing board with a linen shirt before using her eyes to speak eloquently but silently to Lady Eve. "You know," she insinuated. Godfrey grunted.

Lady Eve replied with more than her eyes. "I was hoping you meant something more serious than a simple 'you know.'"

"Madcap heiresses don't do serious." April gulped. A torrid affair seemed risky enough. "Serious" was out of the question. Wasn't it?

"So you're already planning the *end* of Tony?" Lady Eve continued.

Actually April hadn't intended to plan that far ahead when it was so much easier to live in the here and now. Absently she patted Asta's head as he squirmed into her lap. Trust Lady Eve's pragmatic expedience to cut to the heart of the matter.

"Inevitably," she finally conceded with a sigh. A man like Tony would ultimately want a woman with more to give, and so would come the inevitable end.

"Not necessarily," Lady Eve said, taking the oxfords and loafers and low-heeled pumps Godfrey handed her one at a time and tucking them into a zippered accessory bag.

It wasn't a question, but the statement forced April to confront herself anyway. She looked inward at the mass of insecurities her failed marriage had wrought on her heart and faced the truth.

The end was inevitable only if she allowed it to be so. She could define Tony's "I love you" as a sincere expression of his feelings for her, not as an attempt to chain her down.

Though the prospect was daunting, it was possible— just. But did she dare risk her own heart in return?

A CLAMOR OF WHISTLES, sirens and bells accompanied the jingle of spilling coins. Someone whooped in the background.

"Sounds like you've hit the jackpot," Tony said disconsolately into the telephone. He was still in a mood from April's abrupt rejection.

"Sonovagun if it wasn't the slot machine right next to mine," Rocco replied. Now that the jackpot winner had moved on, Tony could hear his uncle inserting quarters and pulling a handle. The machine whirred. Rocco groaned. "Just my luck."

"I thought you said playing the slots is a loser's game."

"It is," Rocco admitted, audibly committing a few more coins to the casino's building fund. "But not when you're flat broke and desperate," he qualified. "I'm down to the little paper cup of quarters the hotel gave me at check-in." The slot machine whirred to another mismatched result.

"Otherwise known as chump change," Tony said. "Isn't it time to move on to the resort in Mexico?"

"Tomorrow. I'll definitely go tomorrow."

"Think bikinis," Tony suggested. Rocco grunted. "By the way, Miss Estelle sends her regards."

"Yeah?"

"She's terribly lonely without you."

"There's a better chance of me hitting the jackpot than there is of that woman having an emotion." Rocco shook the cup of quarters in anticipation as two bunches of cherries and then yet another lemon came up in the windows. "Blast it anyhow."

"I'll tell Miss Estelle you said so."

"You keep out of my love life, boy, and I'll keep out of yours."

Tony winced. "Seeing as how I don't have one . . ."

"Things haven't worked out between you and the blonde?"

"That should have been obvious from the beginning."

"Huh. So that's why you're so nasty today. Ain't gettin' any."

Tony braced one foot on the edge of the desk and pushed off, propelling his chair backward, ending at the coffee machine. He poured himself a cup so strongly brewed it was as dark as the jungle at midnight. And as black as his mood.

It tasted horrible, but it was keeping his head on straight and his body in a hellish caffeine overdrive that was still better than the alternative. He hadn't yet resorted to the Jim Beam—afraid it would bring on hallucinatory dreams of things he'd never have. Or worse, visions of peacocks. Which was really one and the same, now that he thought about it. He put his heel to the windowsill, whizzed back toward the desk and picked up the phone. "It's more than that," he admitted to his uncle. He heard Rocco, who was down to his next-to-last quarter, pull the handle and lose again.

"Don't tell me you're in love," he said into the cell phone the casino had obligingly supplied. There was a telling silence. "Tony?" Still no response. Rocco chuckled. "Well, this'll make your momma very happy."

"April doesn't have breeder's hips."

"Momma won't like that, but sounds good to me."

"And she currently hates me."

"Even better. Means she's got passion."

"Also she's not the roughing-it type. I don't see her hanging out at Cayaxechun. But she'll get into trouble if she's left behind. Then there's the distraction factor. She's very—*extremely*—distracting. Something I don't need at this point in my career. And she's used to a certain lifestyle. I can't provide it, even when I'm not in Guatemala. She has strange friends, too. She comes complete with a butler. Her closet is bigger than my house. I don't even know what color her eyes are. She's the kind of woman who—"

"Get me Miss Estelle," Rocco said forcefully.

Blinking, Tony recovered himself. "Literally or figuratively?"

"Hell's bells," his uncle erupted, "I'm not asking to marry the woman! I just wanna find out what she's putting in your coffee!"

Groaning lightly, Tony rested his head in his hand, the telephone still at his ear but drooping. "Ain't gettin' any, huh, Unc?"

Rocco's overly robust guffaw was telling in its own way.

TONY HUNG UP after thanking Rocco for his advice about repaying Dunky's bookie. He'd suggested they set up the meeting in a very public place and not linger. Rocco hadn't recognized T-Bone's description; he knew of Eldridge only by reputation.

Although it was a moot point now that the forgery scheme had been foiled, they'd chewed over how it was the thugs had come to be two-timing their regular boss by also reporting to Talon Dunkington. Maybe April's theory was right—Talon had run into them at Windenhall and seized the opportunity since Donkey and the Fogbottom had by then gone missing. If so, she was going to be the only loser in the case, and not having a handle on Talon's potential reaction still bothered Tony. Accustomed to accounting for every ounce of soil at a dig, evaluating and placing every tiny historic clue unearthed, he wanted to see at least the business aspects of the Fogbottom case tied up in a neat package.

Edgily his fingers tapped out a galloping rhythm on the desktop. Maybe that was the only reason he was so out of sorts.

No, dammit, he couldn't even pretend it was.

Unannounced, Miss Estelle came into the office. She was dangling a letter from her fingertips. "This came by personal messenger," she said, extending the envelope. The sunny-meadow-flowery scent of April's perfume hung in the air, producing a pang in Tony's midsection.

Rocco had been on the money in one way: His nephew *was* hopelessly in love.

Miss Estelle peered over the glasses perched on the tip of her skinny nose. "Curiously there's no return address."

And she couldn't stand it. Nonchalantly Tony tossed the envelope aside. "Rocco says hi."

Miss Estelle's face was as animated as granite.

"He's having a high old time in Vegas."

She pushed her glasses up her nose and sniffed.

"I gather the showgirls are in fine form."

The secretary's chin quivered. "One can imagine."

Tony relented. "He'll be back soon, with a sunburn and empty pockets." *And I'll be out of here, with an overlarge fee and a black hole where my heart should be.*

"The office shall be in tip-top shape for his return," Miss Estelle replied, as if there'd been any doubt. In the past few days Tony had completed the few simple tasks Rocco had left for him. They'd seemed as dull as dirt compared to April Pierce-Peacock and the case of the missing Fogbottom.

"Aren't you going to open that?" Miss Estelle prompted with a lift of her scrawny eyebrows. Even that slight show of emotion seemed to agitate her. She picked up a folder and snapped its contents into alignment, then bustled over to the cabinets to file it according to a personal method so meticulous but convoluted that not even Tony could fathom it.

He finally slit the flap and pulled out an invitation on rich ecru vellum, handwritten with the elaborate swirls of fancy calligraphy. Straining to see, Miss Estelle bowed her slim form toward the desk like a sapling in a hurricane. Tony hunched his shoulders to block her view as he deciphered the script. Then he glanced at the secretary, who whipped back toward the files and plucked one out at random. He read the invitation again.

"I'll be..." A smile slowly transformed his face. His sudden laugh was part relief, part anticipation. "I'll be damned!" An immediate need to make vital preparations seized him. He was going to do it up right this time. "If you can't beat 'em, join 'em" would be his motto from now on. Forgetting about the curious secretary, he dropped April's alluring invitation on the desk and left the office without a backward glance.

Miss Estelle waited until she heard the *bing* of the elevator doors before she scurried to the desk. She caressed the thick vellum paper with reverent fingertips as she read the missive inviting Tony to Palace Circle for dinner and a grand seduction.

A grand seduction. The secretary made a very small sighing sound.

After finding the stray peacock feather, Miss Estelle had determined to make a study of April Pierce in order to define "that certain something" the heiress possessed—a quality Estelle knew she lacked. While random good fortune had bestowed money and beauty on her, April also had style, glamour and pizzazz. Though she was a scatterbrain—and Miss Estelle had never had use for scatterbrains—the fact remained that April knew how to live.

And more importantly, she knew how to get her man. Certainly The Madcap Heiress would never toil in an office filing documents while her Mr. Right traveled hundreds of miles away to cavort with showgirls and beach bunnies!

Suddenly the straitlaced secretary crushed the invitation in her fist. Perhaps her brain cells had mutated under the influence of the fumes of expensive perfume, but it now seemed crystal clear to her that she was destined to take a lesson from April Pierce.

Miss Estelle's legendary patience had finally run out.

APRIL HAD NEVER been so nervous.

She wanted the setting for her grand seduction to be ideal, every detail done to perfection. Her toilette had taken hours. She'd bathed, perfumed and powdered, then fussed endlessly over the contents of her closet deciding which ensemble Tony would find most alluring. Costumes had always given her confidence—perhaps because she could play a part instead of relying on a reality that wasn't often, if ever, entirely satisfying.

This evening she'd outdone herself, costumewise. Her selection was a vintage flapper dress, a designer original. It was a luscious slip of a thing, sleeveless and scoop-necked, made of transparent layers of fringed, embroidered and beaded silk in alternating shades of green and blue. Her maquillage was worthy of a professional makeup artist—a pouting red Cupid's-bow mouth, apple-blossom cheeks, disarmingly long eyelashes, smoky Cleopatra eyeliner and shadow. The crowning touches were her marcelled hair and beaded, feathered headpiece.

The house was also ready. Every gilded surface glowed, every crystal facet glittered, every mirror gleamed. Extravagant floral arrangements had been delivered early that afternoon and distributed throughout under the direction of Lady Eve before she'd left for the airport with Asta tucked into a carry-on bag. April had called for a limousine because Godfrey, who also doubled as the chauffeur, couldn't leave the kitchen.

Godfrey had been moping and absorbed with the menu all day—moping because of Lady Eve's departure, absorbed because, in spite of himself, he was at heart a Cordon Bleu wanna-be. Despite April's suggestions, he'd decided on nouvelle Alsatian. She was dubious, but willing to cede control . . . in the kitchen.

The doorbell chimed precisely at eight. The butterflies in the pit of April's stomach migrated north. She swallowed them and trip-trapped through the foyer in a pair of aqua silk shoes with arrowhead toes and narrow spike heels, pausing at the Chippendale mirror to check her face. She inserted a cigarette in the long jeweled cigarette holder she was using as a prop. Suddenly stricken with the insight that all her preparations were just so much frou-frou but that it was too late to change things now, she opened the door.

Her giggle was high-pitched with nerves, shaky with relief. Thank God!

Tony had gotten into it!

He smiled wickedly and her knees went weak. He was holding a frilly heart-shaped box of chocolates. Debonair in a white dinner jacket, he had his black hair slicked straight back from his forehead. He looked suave, sophisticated, devastatingly sexy. He could've been Humphrey Bogart in *Casablanca* or Cary Grant in *To Catch A Thief,* but for the tiny diamond glinting in one earlobe. She stared, wide-eyed. The unexpected diamond and the dark glitter of his eyes bumped him up into the dangerous lady-killer category.

From her expertly waved head to her pointy toes, April was thrilled.

Tony's black brows arched. "Lola?"

She shook her head and accepted the candy, deciding on the spur of the moment that this was one time she wanted to be no one but herself. "Just April."

He smiled in approval, his teeth very white. "'Just April' is more than enough for me."

She believed he meant it. Perhaps one day soon it would also be enough for her.

They went into the salon, which was all pink and plush and glowing. Godfrey, resplendent in white gloves, black tie and tails, arrived with a silver salver of crudités. He tugged on his waistcoat and very nearly clicked his heels. April and Tony exchanged amused smiles when he pivoted crisply and whisked silently out of the room. Apparently the proper British influence of Lady Eve Beamish still lingered.

Elegantly April waved the cigarette holder at the blank space over the pink marble mantel. "I'll be so relieved when the Fogbottom is back in its proper place."

Tony glanced at the empty hook. "Donkey simply plucked the painting off the wall and walked out with it? He must have been praying you'd find him straightaway."

"I suspect so. Actually turning the forgery over to his sister was probably a last resort."

"I've been wondering why Talon would take such a risk. The gallery appeared to be thriving at the opening we attended."

"Then you didn't notice how few Sold stickers there were on the paintings." April switched the holder to her left hand and picked up some kind of celery thingy garnished with a glutinous purple glob. Talking about the case was good; it broke the ice. "I wondered, too, but Dunky explained that their father has been funding the gallery. Much as they complain about him, both Talon and Dunky are desperate to gain his approval. So now MacArthur's threatening to kick Talon off the gravy train unless Galerie Diabolique begins to show a profit, and Talon will resort to anything."

"I see." Tony watched April nibble, swallow and lick her lips. It was excruciating torture when he didn't yet dare to grab her, bend her back over his arm and kiss her senseless. "So how was it again that Talon wound up in cahoots with the thugs?"

"Well, I think they were working both ends at once. They probably met Talon when they were hired by Dunky's bookie to scare him into payment—" Worked up, she waved her hands around excitedly. "And then Talon hired them to find Dunky for *her!* She knew he'd snitched the Fogbottom to copy it, but then he disappeared when he got cold feet about going through with the deal!"

"You're going to put someone's eye out," Tony said. After taking the cigarette holder away from her, his hand lingered on hers.

Her eyes, the deep blue of carat-rich gemstones, shone at him as their fingers laced. "Talon must be told that the jig is up. I hope she doesn't try anything stupid before we get Dunky home safely..." Her voice faded away.

"Can we find something besides the case to talk about?" Tony asked.

She made a Mona Lisa smile. "Such as?"

"Such as—" He moved a little closer and said softly, "What exactly a grand seduction entails."

April leaned against him cozily, but she didn't look him in the eye. "For one thing, I promise not to run away this time."

Tony felt a slight tremor ripple through her slender body. He wanted to ask her what had changed her mind, but Godfrey, he of the impeccable timing, entered the salon to announce dinner.

April jumped up and pulled Tony to his feet, smiling with delight as she said, "The Grand Seduction, Rule One... The way to a man's heart is through his stomach." With a red-tipped finger, she traced the shape of a heart above Tony's black satin cummerbund, then spun away to lead him into the dining room that adjoined the salon, her hips swinging. His eyes narrowed when he saw that her dress was essentially backless. A long rope of pearls interspersed with sapphires swayed between her bare shoulder blades.

The table was elaborately furbished with china, silver, linen, Gothic candelabra and glorious clouds of pink camellias. They sat to a first course of oysters on grilled potato slices, artistically arranged around radicchio and endive salad. Godfrey opened and poured the Alsatian Riesling, then exited, his tread becoming audible. April cast a brief worried glance after him.

Tony examined his plate. "Oysters?"

"Better than garlic," was her lighthearted gibe.

"But in this case, not necessary," he returned wickedly.

She toasted him with her glass of white wine. "So glad to hear it!"

Their laughter dissolved any remaining tension. Halfway through the main course of lamb, fresh morels and asparagus, they were too busy talking to notice the doorbell. There was a commotion in the foyer, then suddenly Talon Dunkington barged through the salon and into the dining room, her color high and her voice demanding. Godfrey had one hand on the back of the studded leather belt that cinched her Hell's-Angels-do-haute-couture metal mesh minidress, but Talon was doing more towing than he was restraining.

"Where is Dunky?" she screeched.

April's fingers fluttered nervously. "I couldn't say."

"You must know, seeing as how you're such good pals with the fool," Talon sneered. She wrenched out of Godfrey's grasp and ungracefully plunked herself into a chair. Her chest heaved. "I have to find him. Immediately. It's an emergency!"

Tony cocked his head. "But something tells me you would be just as satisfied with the Fogbottom."

Nostrils flaring, Talon confronted him with suspicion. "Who the hell are you? What would you know about the Fogbottom?" She snatched up April's glass and swallowed a healthy gulp of wine. "Oh, the private investigator," she remembered, and helped herself to more wine straight from the bottle. "Well, what good are you if you can't even track down my dear idiot scaredy-pants brother?"

"Who says I haven't?" Tony asked.

April rescued the bottle before their uninvited guest could drain it. She passed it to Godfrey for safekeeping. "Talon—"

Talon's ebony eyes darted between her and Tony. "Where is he, then?" she shouted, slamming her palms on the table. She'd lost all restraint. "I must have that painting as soon as possible or my father will—*hic*—close the gallery!"

"You're drunk," April accused.

"And disorderly," added Tony.

"Should I ring up the authorities, mum?" inquired Godfrey.

"Doesn't anyone answer the door in this place?" Miss Estelle demanded, striding into the room. Her forehead was furrowed beneath a wide-brimmed straw hat with a peacock feather stuck in the brim. "I assure you I rang the bell *and* knocked. Several times." She didn't appreciate having to break etiquette.

"Miss Estelle?" Tony was amazed.

April grinned. "You look fetching."

She was wearing an ivory dress with a shantung rose-patterned jacket. Her narrow feet, planted in a V, sported open-toed pumps decorated with pink silk roses. "I have an urgent message from Rocco. I mean, ahem, Mr. Farentino." She flushed and pressed her precisely lipsticked lips together in a prim line.

"Big whoop-de-do," Talon said soupily. "What about me?"

Miss Estelle glanced down her nose at the drunken, harried-looking creature lolling at the table and without a word dismissed Talon as beneath contempt. "Rocco called a few hours after you left the office," she said, addressing Tony. "Apparently he cashed in his airplane ticket, gambled the money away and is presently stuck in Las Vegas without a cent to his name."

April was yanking camellias out of the centerpiece. "You must have a corsage, Miss Estelle. Please fetch me some tape and a few pins, Godfrey."

The lovelorn butler shrugged. "Whatever you say."

Tony didn't get it. "Why does she need—"

"Tony, darling, I suggest you concentrate on solving Rocco's problem. Maybe Gamblers Anonymous will give a group discount if we enroll him and Dunky."

Miss Estelle waved a vinyl-bound ledger. She was positively giddy with the rashness of her intentions. "I've already liberated the firm's checkbook. If you'll just okay the transaction, Mr. Farentino, I can dispatch a money order to Rocco within the hour."

April had fashioned a make-do corsage. Her back turned to Tony, she pinned it to Miss Estelle's shoulder and winked in woman-to-woman conspiracy. "Go for it, Lola," she whispered.

Miss Estelle's answering smile was tremulous but hopeful.

Talon jerked to attention. "Paris is burning," she announced dramatically, then collapsed, her head slamming down among the cutlery.

"My strudel!" Godfrey bellowed, and *clump-clump-clumped* double-time to the kitchen. Wisps of smoke curled from the doorway.

The acrid scent of burning pastry wafted into the dining room as the sudden, piercing chorus of all seven downstairs smoke detectors split the air.

9

A Grand Time Is—Still—Had By All

BY THE TIME the detectors had been turned off, the fire department called off and a semblance of order restored, the plucked centerpiece had collapsed and the dozen candles of the candelabra had burned down to nubs and were guttering out one by one. April regarded the wreckage of her lovely table and turned away in dismay.

Having disposed of the blackened plum strudels and aired out the kitchen, Godfrey was discharged with orders to deliver Talon to Windenhall and Miss Estelle to whatever destination she might choose. Tony took the butler aside and urged him to take his time.

Meanwhile, April gave up on dessert when she found the crystal glasses and ice-bucketed bottle of champagne Godfrey had set at the ready before the various calamities and distractions had occurred. She fished the bottle out of several inches of water and carried it, dripping and tepid, into the salon.

Tony was on the sofa, patiently awaiting the commencement of the truncated grand seduction.

April managed a brave smile as she held up the bottle and clinked the accompanying flutes. "This has been a Titanic of an evening. It seems only appropriate that we should christen it with champagne."

He murmured dissent. "My hopes haven't been entirely dashed, but..."

"But what?" she asked, almost afraid of what disaster might strike next. It was tornado season, after all.

The deepening of Tony's dimple alerted her otherwise. "Is that an iceberg looming behind you?"

Reflexively she glanced back, then, with a dry laugh, slid onto the sofa beside him. "I wouldn't be surprised. Anything less and the grand seduction would be disappointingly incomplete."

He used his fingertip to outline a heart over her left breast. "Take heart, April Peacock. All is not lost."

Her pulse quickened. "But I wanted everything to be so nice. So perfect."

"It's certainly been memorable." With his fingers at her jaw, he turned her face and brushed her lips with a kiss. "Let's try for unforgettable." His second kiss lingered. "Shall I open the champagne?"

"I can do it," April insisted breathlessly. She peeled off the foil with the bottle resting in her lap. Peeping up at Tony through the drooping feathers and fringe of her flapper headpiece, she tugged on the cork. It burst free, shooting toward the ceiling like a missile. A blast of champagne spurted from the mouth of the bottle; April shrieked as it sprayed her in the face.

Too late, Tony grabbed the frothing bottle and tipped it toward the waiting flutes. Beads of champagne dripped off April's nose and chin. The sparkling liquid momentarily pooled in her lap, then seeped between her thighs onto the sofa, making damp patches on the velvet.

"Oh...no...oh...no..." She blinked her spangled lashes, her expression of dismay a perfect match for her melted maquillage. "Oh, no!" There didn't seem to be anything else to say.

Tony pulled a black silk square from his pocket and tried to contain the damage. Making odd chuffing noises, she ducked her head and dived for the shelter of his chest. He patted her back. "That's okay, April. What's a grand seduction without an impromptu champagne shower?'' She breathed raggedly against his jacket, sounding on the verge of tears. ''Don't cry,'' he soothed.

''I never cry.'' With that, she popped up, proclaimed, ''This may not have been grand, but it's certainly been madcap!'' and burst into gulping, hiccuping, near-hysterical laughter. She tore off her headpiece and whipped her head from side to side, sprinkling Tony with droplets.

''Whoops—your jacket.'' A smeared replica of April's painted face had stained its pristine front. Giggling at the incongruity, she used his sleeve to wipe away the rest of her makeup, then finished the mop-up with the silk square. She dabbed at her eyes and blew her nose. By the time she was finished, he was almost as big a mess as she.

''Well,'' she said, drawing a deep, calming breath as she plucked at the bodice of her clinging dress.

Tony slipped out of his ruined dinner jacket. ''You know, I think I like you better this way.''

She rose from the sofa. ''The drowned-rat look does things for you?''

He took a handful of her skirt and tugged her over to stand before him. She struggled to keep her knees from buckling as one of his hands inched under the fringed layers of her dress and the other found the bare skin of her back. He turned his face up to hers, the cleft in his chin hovering near her belly button. His dark eyes were the sexiest she'd ever seen. The small of her back tingled beneath his palm.

''I think it's the no-more-heiress look that does it.''

Her answering smile was feeble. ''Nothing a hot shower won't cure.''

''I was hoping you'd say that.''

Before April fully realized what was happening, Tony had raised the hem of the dress above her waist. Her mouth dropped open as he kept going, standing as he lifted the yards of damp silk right up off over her head. After he tossed the dress aside, April stood before him in nothing but pearls, shoes, hose and the lacy aqua garter belt that matched her silk French-cut panties.

Her cheeks flamed pink. Though the rest of her body was still chilled from the drenching, that changed soon enough as Tony's gaze meandered over her near-nude form. Heat accompanied the path of his eyes, flushing her torso, warming her thighs, pooling in the recesses of her lower body just like the champagne. Clenching her muscles, April stood frozen when his mouth quirked at the sight of her bare breasts and the tight pink circles of her nipples, puckered from the wet and cold but blossoming voluptuously under the steam-heat of his appraisal.

April wanted to curl up in mortification but at the same time she wanted to make a flying leap into Tony's arms. She held her ground, though never having felt so intensely, erotically appreciated, *never* having wanted a man so much.

She quivered when he reached for her, but instead of touching bared skin he hooked one finger around the pearls looped across her collarbone and pulled them slowly, slowly from back to front. The ivory globes rolled smoothly across her flesh. Desire pulsed through her with each beat of her heart. She licked her suddenly dry lips. "Oh," she whispered, swaying toward him, "Oh, Tony..."

The warm pearls and cold sapphires slid over her breasts, buffeting her nipples with little shocks at each contact. Unable to take the slow torture any longer, April skated her hands up her ribs, catching and holding her breasts, pressing her palms tight against them as if that could contain her immense need for Tony's touch. "I can't—" she cried.

He swooped her into his arms, his mouth covering hers in an instant. His kiss, so fierce and deep, assured her that his need matched her own. She clutched his arms, his shoulders, then his hair, grasping and greedy and amazed that she'd ever been foolish enough to force him away.

Tony tore his mouth from hers. "I have to tell you," he said, his breath hot and panting, his eyes as dark as night, "I have to tell you I love you." He smoothed damp curling strands of hair away from her face and looked into her eyes. "I love you no matter how much it scares you."

April expected the dreaded phrase to drop through the hollow space inside her and crash spectacularly against the raging strength of their physical attraction. She tensed, waiting. Nothing. Tony pressed soft kisses onto the open O of her lips. Still nothing but desire. Desire and something more. Warmth, she thought. Pleasure. Her heart swelled with emotion. Maybe even . . . love.

She tilted her head back, her face wreathed with joy. Tony's tongue swiped across her throat, his lips nibbled the side of her neck. "Please, Tony, darling Tony," she sang. "Make love to me now."

"Yes," he promised. "But we'd better get upstairs while we're still ambulatory."

"And before Godfrey gets back!" They ran for the stairs like a couple of naughty teenagers, scrambling up them with only one or two pit stops of urgent demand. Lake Michigan glinted a deep midnight blue outside the window at the landing. April had her cheek pressed tight against the mullioned glass as Tony rained kissed along her spine and slowly slid his hand down the back of her panties. Neither of them appreciated the view.

April did come back to awareness long enough to contend with the studs of his dress shirt. She peeled it back from his honey brown chest as he half lifted, half pushed her up the dais of her bed. They collapsed onto it, arms around each other, legs intertwined. Tony unsnapped the garter, his fingers gently smoothing the flesh of her thighs, and April discarded her panties with a flamboyant kick that would have done a showgirl proud.

Where was her awkwardness? She wondered, stroking her fingers through the black hair dusted across his chest, making him groan when she tweaked one of his flat brown nipples. Why wasn't she fumbling with incompetence?

Tony was licking at the stickiness of the champagne that had soaked through her bodice. He twirled the rope of pearls around her breasts with one hand, petted with the other. His mouth was hot as it covered her breast and pulled on the flesh with a deep, sexual hunger. His teeth raked her nipple. April squirmed. She bit her lip. Finally she gave up on decorum and vocalized, in a keening howl, the overwhelming pleasure surging through her.

"I like a woman who knows how to howl," Tony said, his eyes dancing as he reached up for her. "Can you make me howl?" he asked against her lips before he started to kiss her again.

Her answer was delayed for at least five minutes. "I can try," she said, almost comically resolute despite her kiss-swollen lips.

"This is not a test," Tony assured her as she pushed at his chest and he obediently rolled onto his back.

No, it wasn't, she happily acknowledged. How wonderful!

She was a bit awkward in unzipping and removing his pants. He didn't seem to mind, however, and he only smiled when she regarded the daunting sight of his tight black briefs and the formidable bulge they contained as if she needed instructions on the proper procedure before continuing. "Improvise," he suggested, but in the end he helped, which it turned out was quite okay, too, as he put his hand over hers and guided the way. He was patient, though clinging to the last vestiges of his self-control, as she explored his reactions to each of her tentative touches and strokes. When all her experiments seemed to meet with success, she became bolder. She wound the pearls around his erection and used both hands, all her fingers, then her lips and, gently, her teeth.

Tony howled.

April liked it.

She liked it even more when he told her through gritted teeth that she was a little *too* adept and she'd have to stop before he did more than howl. So she curled up beside him and matched her lips to his in long, sweet, succulent kisses that seemed to last forever. April was amazed not only by the strength of their mutual desire, but at how wonderful it made her feel. How loved.

"I didn't think I could risk this without being—" she caught her breath when Tony cupped his hand between her thighs "—The—Madcap—Heiress," she finished, each word accompanied by a gasp as his fingers stroked through her liquid warmth.

"Why not?" he asked. "You'd have to be a risk-taker to invent The Madcap Heiress in the first place." His low voice resonated in the frissons racing over the surface of her skin.

He moved over her, nudging her thighs wider apart. April closed her eyes, her senses reeling, her mind floating free. "Loving you is the biggest risk I've ever taken," she whispered, and her voice seemed to come from someplace very far away.

His body, poised with strained muscles as it slowly sank into hers, made the promise even before the words were said. "It's a sure thing," he panted, finding her very tight even though he knew she was more than ready. She tilted her hips, and she reached up to latch on to the lacquered black curves of the headboard. He gained the last inch.

Tony unclenched her tight grip and gently brought her hands down to his shoulders. He pulled her legs up, his hands on the back of her thighs, and she instinctively coiled them around him as he made a first, tentative, exquisite thrust.

April's eyelids popped open as a pinpoint of intense pleasure flared to life. Sinuously Tony moved inside her. The pinpoint flowered into a most delicious sizzle of sensation. Her body flowed with its heat.

She skimmed her hands down his flexing shoulders to his hips, testing their movement and finding she could match the rhythm. She also found that by swiveling her hips and tightening muscles she'd scarcely been aware of having, she could make him shudder and call her name.

Soon she was not thinking so clearly. Her desire was beyond extreme, her body's aching need for completion was all-consuming.

She was on the brink of losing control.

Before she could react with her usual apprehension, a deep thrust from Tony pushed her over the edge. She soared with her explosive climax, astonished and almost afraid, but loving it just the same. In a shaky voice, she called Tony's name again and again until it was a part of her.

Tony quickened his pace, at last seeking his own release. It came over him in a torrent, washing through him and into April. She bit back his hoarse cry with her kiss, tenderly caressing his face with her lips as he sank, sated, into her waiting arms.

DECADENTLY NUDE AND INDOLENT, April lay on her stomach on the tousled bed, eating chocolates. Tony was stretched out beside her—long, broad, tan and muscular, utterly masculine against the lace of the coverlet and the ivory satin of the sheets. She checked him out, not bothering to be discreet about it since his eyes were closed. Smiling with satisfaction, she rummaged through the heart-shaped candy box. "Not bad for my first time."

Startled from sleep, Tony's shoulders jerked off the pillow. "Not—"

April dropped a half-eaten butternut cream back into the box. "Well, no, I actually meant my first *one*."

He twirled his finger. "Your first..."

"Uh-huh. Freeman swore I was frigid."

"Guess he must've missed the saying about there being no frigid women, only inept men, huh?" Tony's eyes narrowed. "But what about the others?"

"What others?"

He blinked in amazement. "No others?" April shook her head, her sapphire eyes glinting. "Wow," he breathed. "That's..." He thought about it for a moment, with a growing sense of male pride and possessiveness. "That's great."

She nodded wisely. "It is now."

He sank back and closed his eyes, extremely contented. "So you hit the jackpot. I guess congratulations are in order."

She beamed through a mouthful of chocolate. "No, I believe the congratulations go to you, darling Tony. For being so fabulously *ept*."

Grinning to himself, he opened his eyes a crack. April was licking her fingers, both legs bent at the knee and swaying back and forth, crisscrossing over the long pink-and-white curve of her bare flanks. One of the sheer white lengths of fabric that had been draped across the sleek posts of the bed frame had *somehow* worked itself loose. It was now draped like a veil across April's head and shoulders.

"You look like a bride," he said softly.

A gentle expression flitted over her face before she tossed her head and sat up, gaily twining the transparent silk around her head and neck and breasts. "A very well-used one!" she agreed, and reached again for her sweets.

He watched her rustle through the remains. "I should have known you'd be the type to nibble every chocolate in the box."

"I was born to nibble—" she winked "—chocolates." She set the box on her lap. "But I like the soft centers, not the chewy ones. You can have all the caramels." She popped one into his mouth, then nuzzled his ear while he chewed.

He winced. "Ouch."

Her tongue flicked the diamond in his earlobe. "That hurts?"

"Seeing as how I had a hole punched in my ear at a shopping mall just a few hours ago, yeah, it hurts."

She giggled. "Poor Tony."

His chest shook with barely contained laughter. "Earlier, I'd decided that I was going to suggest you call me Mario."

"Mario," she mused. "You mean Mario as in Lola, the blond bombshell, and Mario, her suave boyfriend?"

"Yup."

She touched the tiny diamond with her fingertip. It was sexy, but it wasn't purely Tony... "I'll bet not many archaeologists wear earrings."

"There might be a few," he hedged. "Anyway, the Mayans were heavily into body-piercing—and not just earlobes, if you know what I mean. Talk about ouch."

She shook her head, chiding him with a look. "Why don't you take it out? I'm sure the hole will still grow in."

"I thought you'd like it."

"I sort of do, but I like Tony Farentino even more. If you know what I mean?"

"Mmm." He sneaked one finger in between the layers of silk wound around her torso then pulled down, revealing a small bare breast. "Just as I prefer one hundred percent pure April Pierce."

"Oh, that's nice." She sighed.

"That?" His fingertip brushed her pebbled nipple. "Or this?"

"Anything." She flung herself into his arms, scattering chocolates and their tiny pleated paper cups all over the bed. "And everything—absolutely everything!"

Regardless of the squashed chocolates, he held her tight. "Then let's go for orgasm number two. And, hell, why not number three while we're at it?"

"Hoo-wheeee," April whooped out of sheer exuberance. "Why, Tony, you're not just a man, you're a *Legend!*"

"BUCKINGHAM FOUNTAIN. Grant Park. Six p.m."

April synchronized her wristwatch. "Check."

"Gimme a break," Tony muttered, making a face at her beneath a limb of the tree she was using as camouflage. "This isn't an undercover operation."

They were at the park for the meeting with the thugs. After they handed over the money Donkey owed to the bookie, he would no longer be in danger of having his fingers snapped like twigs. He could come out of hiding at last, and bring the original Fogbottom with him. Once they were all safe, Tony was determined to look into installing a state-of-the-art alarm system at April's town house.

"*Mario* would've been willing to wear a trench coat and fedora," she was complaining. "Where is he when I need him?" She peered around the trunk. "Please get back to your position before the thugs arrive."

"I don't see the point when they already know we're meeting them here with the money."

"Eldridge might pull a dirty trick. Better to be cautious than to find ourselves double-crossed."

"Listen, April, I checked out this whole setup with Rocco. He swears we'll be perfectly safe as long as we hand over the cash as promised. Donkey's bookie only wants what he's owed and the thugs follow his orders. There'll be no scenes, fights or gunplay." Tony would never have let April in on the deal—even if it was her money they were delivering to settle Donkey's gambling debt—if he hadn't been assured by Rocco that there was practically no chance of the transaction going sour.

"They've exhibited a propensity for scheming," she persisted. "Have you forgotten that they were also working for Talon until just recently? Who knows what she's plotting now that Dunky won't be delivering the forged Fogbottom—oh, look!" April scurried a few yards to the left and ducked behind a park bench. She beckoned him to join her, whispering sharply, "T-Bone at three o'clock!"

Covertly she peeked past the bench. Tony strolled over and sat on it in plain sight. T-Bone was ambling over a section of green lawn, holding a rainbow snow cone in one huge fist; a cigarette dangled from the corner of his mouth. "No sign of Eldridge," she said triumphantly. "See, I told you so. They're up to dirty tricks."

Tony hated to burst her bubble, but . . . "Eldridge is already waiting at the fountain. Impatiently, I might add."

She swiveled on her heels, then slowly rose to full height. In an effort to blend with the tourists, she'd worn a Cubs' baseball cap, a Bulls' NBA Championship T-shirt, baggy shorts and a fanny pack. An expensive Leica hung around her neck. "Well, shoot," she said. As if that had given her an idea, she aimed the camera.

He put his hand over the lens. "Not a good idea, April. Let's just get this over with, okay? No dramatics, no scenes and definitely *no Lola.*"

Disgusted, she shoved the bill of the cap up her forehead. "I'm starting to think you should've kept the earring."

"Number six tonight," he said ultracasually. Four and five had come that morning as they'd alternated between the shower, the bed and back to the shower.

"Check," she replied with an appreciative chuckle.

"Be good, now," he warned as they approached the large fountain.

Eldridge's narrow face with its puckered scar and perpetual sneer looked abnormally pale in the bright sunshine. "Look, Bone, if it ain't the pool shark." His gaze crawled over April. "And the Pierce broad. Dammit, girl, you drive like a maniac."

"Thank you," she said precisely, obviously pleased.

"Me and Bone have decided to let you two amateurs off easy so long as you got the money Dunkington owes us."

"We've got it," Tony said, slipping off his blue nylon knapsack.

"Cash?" Eldridge snatched the knapsack, unzipped it and set it on the ledge of the fountain. He fingered the contents, licking his lips greedily.

"Lemme see." T-Bone thrust his rainbow-stained hand into the maw of the knapsack.

Eldridge slapped his hand. "You're getting it all sticky."

"But I never seen a hunnert and fifty—"

Eldridge grabbed for the knapsack as T-Bone leaned over to look inside. Their skulls smashed together like battling mountain goats. T-Bone's burning cigarette dropped out of his open mouth, flipped past the gaping zipper and onto the pile of cash. The lit end scorched a hole through the top layer of a packet of hundreds.

"You big dumb hunk of meat!" Eldridge yelled. "You've set the money on fire!"

T-Bone rubbed the top of his skull. "It wasn't my fault. You bonked me on the head."

"You bonked me," Eldridge insisted. He made a fist.

T-Bone made two fists.

"Now, boys," April clucked, eyeing the unzipped pack warily. There was more smoke than ought to come from one cigarette. When a small flickering flame appeared, she darted between the scowling thugs and pushed the knapsack into the fountain with a splash. Aghast, the thugs watched as it sank to the bottom among a copper and silver constellation of tourist-tossed coins.

"Whatchoo do that for?" T-Bone asked.

"Now the money's all soggy," Eldridge whined.

"At least the fire is out," April said smugly.

Tony grabbed her hand and started dragging her away from the thugs despite her voluble protests—something about offering T-Bone a job. "Move it," he growled. "Now."

She pulled up stubbornly. "What makes you think you can order me—" A strange look came over her face. Tony waited until she finally nodded. "Okay, I'll go with you."

"Then do it fast, but don't run," he said under his breath. Looping his arm around her waist to make them look like innocuous tourists on a stroll in the park, he hustled her along, daring one backward glance once they'd rounded a fence. T-Bone was holding the back of Eldridge's belt, restraining him from falling into the water as the smaller thug stretched over the ledge to fish the nylon knapsack out of the fountain. They were totally oblivious to the suspicious regard of an approaching police officer.

"Sorry if I was bossy," Tony said when they were safely away. "Thanks for trusting me."

"I did, didn't I?" April was pleased with herself. "I decided you must have had a very good reason for ordering me around, so I went along with you." Her shoulders stiffened. "I assume there *is* an appropriate explanation."

He told her about the policewoman. Immediately she wanted to run back to defend the thugs' honor—or at least T-Bone's. "He'd be all right if I could just get him away from Eldridge's influence. He'd make a good bodyguard."

"You don't need a bodyguard," Tony said cautiously. Not as long as she had *him*, which would be a long time if he had anything to say about it.

"No, I suppose not." She brightened. "But maybe I could get Godfrey's old job for T-Bone."

"Oh?"

She nodded enthusiastically. "Bouncer at Monkey-shines. That was how I met Godfrey, when the Pranksters were getting tossed out for smashing our champagne glasses on the dance floor."

Tony steered her along the sidewalk. "Aha. Your butler was once a bouncer. Why am I not surprised?"

"He had been a roadie on the Stones' last North American tour. Mick fired him after some silly accident with a forty-thousand-dollar guitar, so Godfrey was stranded in Illinois without a proper green card and he—whoops, I wasn't supposed to mention that part of it."

"Oh, God."

"His talents were obviously going to waste, booting drunken rich kids out of Monkeyshines," April continued cheerfully. "I had just bought my house, so I hired him as a butler. Every madcap heiress needs an English butler, you know."

"Oh, God, Godfrey's an illegal alien."

"There is a way to solve that." She smiled slyly. "I'd thought to send him on to Lady Eve in London. Kind of a living thank-you present."

Tony halted in the middle of the foot traffic. People surged around him. "I get the feeling Godfrey wouldn't object, but what are you thanking Lady Eve for?"

"Oops." April clapped her hand over her mouth. "That was something else I wasn't supposed to mention. At least not yet."

"Don't tell me." He held up his hands, warding her off as she came at him. "Do not tell me. I absolutely don't want to know."

She pushed her camera aside and slipped her hands around his waist. "That's okay. You'll find out soon enough and, believe me, you *do* want to know." Her fingers crossed. "I hope."

Tony's head tilted back as he looked up at the sky beseechingly. "Somebody please save me from this woman."

She rose on her toes to kiss the dent in his chin. "Not a chance, buster—in heaven or in hell. You'll never get away from The Madcap Heiress."

He kissed her back, hoping she meant it.

10

The Real Thing

"WHO NEEDS CHAMPAGNE?"

April didn't realize she'd spoken the thought aloud; the effervescence of vintage Tony was once again fizzling through her bloodstream, deluging every inch of her in wave after sparkling wave. She braced her arms, hands splayed on his chest, and rode the crest of pure sensation until it hurled her into the spectacular whirlpool of another climax. She stiffened, head flung back, mouth open and gasping, then gradually slumped forward, utterly satiated.

"April." Tony's hands tightened on her waist, holding her astride him as he pumped up into her, his hips lifting both of them inches off the bed. *"April."*

"Yes, Tony." She curled down over him as his body quieted, slithering sexily against his sweat-damp skin. Her palms massaged the tight muscles in his shoulders and upper arms. Cheek to hairy chest, skin to pungent skin, she lay atop him, luxuriating in their closeness.

Eyes closed, his head lolled on the pillow. "You're going to kill me. Must you do everything to excess?"

"Of course. After all, I haven't yet lost count."

Lazily he dropped his hand over her derriere and tucked her a little tighter into the warm notch between his thighs. She nestled against him with a sigh of complete contentment. "Before you finish me off," he murmured, "what was that about the champagne?"

She lifted her head, blinking drowsily. "Just that I'm drunk on you, Tony darling." She rested her chin on his breastbone and smiled the big, goofy smile of the happily intoxicated. "Well and truly inebriated."

Returning her cheek to his chest, she listened to the slowing cadence of his heart. She'd never had this kind of closeness with Freeman. He'd always withdrawn immediately after sex, leaving April alone in bed, feeling unsatisfied and, despite the oft-repeated "I love you's," desperately unloved.

Now, even the words were nice to hear, coming from Tony. But he'd also made her understand how little they meant when they weren't backed up by thought and deed and honest emotion. Although April sincerely hoped that she was capable of returning the favor, she wasn't yet certain. There was still something holding her back. Or something she was holding back.

"Having noticed how much you like your champagne, I'm taking that as a huge compliment," Tony murmured.

She stirred. "It's hard to maintain the proper madcap attitude without an equivalent amount of champagne, so... Mimosas, champagne cocktails, Dom Pérignon by the magnum and Cristal by the jeroboam." Yikes—enough to float a boat. She'd never added it up before! "Really, I'd much rather be addicted to the taste of you, Tony. As long as my supply doesn't run out."

Or run to Cayaxechun? "There's not much champagne in Guatemala," he said, tiptoeing around the subject.

"I wouldn't expect so."

"In fact, once at the site, there's very little to speak of in the way of creature comforts of any sort."

"Mmm. And we both know I'm a *very* decadent creature," she replied, her voice blurred by sleepiness so he couldn't decide whether or not she'd been teasing.

Either way, it was true. So, okay, he'd have to learn to work around that fact. Maybe. Somehow. But what if April was extending a subtle warning? What if she meant that he shouldn't expect her to even try? He wasn't going to give up his madcap heiress now that he understood how much more there was to her than that, and he wasn't interested in a long-distance relationship, so all that remained was for him to sacrifice certain career ambitions. Could he do that?

For April—beautiful, kind, funny, frightened, vulnerable April—the answer was most definitely *yes*.

Thirty minutes later, they'd showered, dressed and consumed a quick breakfast of granola cereal. Since Eldridge had smooth-talked his way out of Grant Park with the waterlogged knapsack, Chicago was once again safe for Dunky's return. They were planning to drive north, break the good news to Dunky and escort the Fogbottom back to its rightful place above April's mantel. Privately, Tony also intended to see the fake Fogbottom destroyed—even if he had to toss it into Veronica Lake.

"Let's get going," he urged, watching April fuss with the waistband of her brown leopard-print shorts and shirt. Somewhere between the bed and the breakfast table, her eyes had turned chocolate brown. He'd yet to catch her at it. "We've got a long drive."

"Oh, look, mail," she said once they were finally making their way to the front door. The morning delivery had fanned out on the rug beneath the mail slot. April gathered it up, handed it over, then noticed a colorful card sticking out from between a starchy business envelope and an anthropology journal. She snatched it up. "A postcard from Vegas."

He tried to grab it, but she danced away down the hall, waving it gleefully. "Rocco and Miss Estelle got married!"

"No." Tony was stunned. April was not.

"Yes, it's true. I knew it, I knew it!" Chortling, she returned to the message. "Miss Estelle delivered Rocco's rescue money in person. He says absence must have made the heart grow fonder, because she swept him off his feet!"

Tony seized the card. "They were married at the Pair-a-dice Chapel of Love. Appropriate. Miss Estelle worked her usual magic and got Rocco's swinging singles' reservation switched over to a couples' resort. They're honeymooning in Cancún." He read the last line and rolled his eyes. "Rocco wants me to take charge of the office until they get back."

"That's great," April enthused. "I can help."

"No way. I'm an archaeologist, not a sleuth, and it's time we both realized it. I'll close up shop till Rocco gets back."

"But there's a Mario inside of you dying to—"

Oblivious, Tony was staring at the postcard in confusion. He handed it to April. "Look at the signature."

"Rocco and Lola Farentino," she read. "So what?"

"Who's Lola?"

"Miss Estelle, of course. Lola is her first name. Didn't you know that?"

"Lola Estelle?" He shook his head. "I thought Estelle was her first name."

"It's not," April said. "Isn't it perfect? What a coincidence! I told her she should use the name, it would loosen her up and give Rocco a new, nonsecretarial perspective on her possibilities—and I guess she took my advice!"

"Lola Estelle?" he repeated.

"Come to think of it, the names Rocco and Mario are rather similar. I believe their marriage was destined." She sighed. "How perfectly romantic."

"Well, they do make a good team, we already know that," Tony agreed, flipping through the rest of his mail. He stopped at the crisp business envelope. "What's this? The Ferncliffe Foundation?"

April's eyes widened. "So soon?"

He tore it open. "They're offering me the funds to continue the dig at Cayaxechun," he said slowly, as awed by his unexpected good fortune as a naughty boy on Christmas morning. "The Ferncliffe Foundation is one of the most prestigious anthropological organizations in the world. Their grants usually go to internationally important digs—and they want me!" He lifted April off her feet, started to swing her around, then dropped her to re-read the letter and confirm the news. He traced the engraved letterhead, double-checked the London postmark. "It's not a joke. It's true."

"Of course it's true. The Ferncliffe Foundation is lucky to have you," April boasted. "Anyone would be."

"But I didn't even apply—" He looked at April's face, then again at the postmark. He flipped back to the letterhead. "Lady Hortense Ferncliffe Beamish, directress. Lady... Beamish. Do you know something about this?"

She braced herself. "Please don't let foolish, stubborn, male pride get in the way of—"

"Now I know why you're sending Godfrey to Lady Eve."

"Basil Ferncliffe was on Howard Carter's heels when he discovered King Tut's tomb," she explained hastily. "Lady Eve's family started The Ferncliffe Foundation decades ago, and she happens to have a seat on the board." She peeped at his face to see how he was taking it. "I only asked her to look into the possibility of *considering—*"

Tony kissed her to shut her up. It didn't work—or at least not for long. "So you're not too mad at me?" she asked in a thin voice. "I know I shouldn't have interfered, but can you just think of it as networking and accept the—"

He lifted her arms, placed them around his neck and kissed her again. "Of course I'll accept the grant."

"Oh." She patted the back of his head. "That's good, then. I'm glad you're being sensible about this."

"I'm being egotistical. Or confident, anyway." He smiled at her. "I happen to think the work my team was doing at Cayaxechun was good enough, and important enough, to warrant attention from The Ferncliffe Foundation all on its own. If you were the catalyst for getting them to notice us, well . . ." He shrugged. "All I can do is thank my lucky stars." Brushing her hair aside, he spoke one hushed word into her ear: *"Thanks."*

She shivered at the ticklish warmth, the corners of her lips curling. "You're very welcome."

"That seems inadequate, though." He cocked his head, gazing upward as if for inspiration. "If I were actually going to leave, I'd probably have to thank you by hiring T-Bone as Godfrey's replacement."

April started to laugh, then stopped abruptly. "What do you mean *if?*"

"I'm glad that work can continue at Cayaxechun because of the grant, but I won't be changing my personal plans." He watched the play of emotions on her face, waiting for the expected relief to surface. "I'd already decided to stick around. For good. Probably find a college that doesn't mind that my last dig met with a natural disaster before I earned the Archaeologist of the Year trophy."

"But you said—you were so excited—and teaching isn't—" Her bright brown eyes crackled with fiery determination. "Oh, no, you don't, Tony! You're accepting

hat grant for yourself and you're going back to Guatemala and I don't want to hear one word to the contrary."
She stuck her chin in the air and firmed her trembling
lower lip. "I'd rather take T-Bone, as a butler, a bodyguard, even a *nursemaid,* than see you miss this oppor-
unity."

"And I'd rather be with you," he insisted.

She was flattered, but unrelenting. "Well, I'd rather not
have you—that way."

Stubbornly they faced each other in the narrow hallway at Tony's front door, each wanting what was best for
he other. It was a standoff, and neither of them would
give in.

Eventually they had to leave for Wisconsin, still wran-
gling over the subject as they traveled north, too absorbed in the discussion to notice the sports car following
hem. By the time they reached Belle Terre, April was ex-
hausted—not from countering Tony's arguments, but
from waiting on tenterhooks for him to extend a simple
invitation to join him in Guatemala. Which, it seemed to
her, was the obvious solution. Unfortunately, Tony had
gotten some crazy idea about her being too much of a
wimp to take the rigorous environment of Guatemala's
rain forest. Drat that Madcap Heiress—the original
spoiled-deb-delicate-society-princess-cream-puff herself!

April asked Tony to stop at the bakery for éclairs. Once
on the sidewalk, she thought she recognized a sleek black
car easing along the street. By the time she'd removed her
sunglasses for a better look, it had turned the corner.

The thugs had driven a black car. A sedan, she remembered, not a stylish sports car. Anyway, they no longer had
a reason to find Dunky.

April was returning to the convertible with the boxed
éclairs when she thought of the fake Fogbottom, worth
quite a bit of money if it wound up in unscrupulous
hands. She decided not to mention that to Tony.

DUNKY GREETED THEM with an oar in his hands.

"Taken up boating?" Tony asked as he stepped out from the passenger side of the convertible. For reasons that eluded him, April had insisted on driving after their detour to the bakery. It hadn't bothered him to give up the wheel, but he had wondered about her clenched fist on the gearshift and her nervous, darting glances in the rearview mirror. Remembering previous excursions, he'd buckled his seat belt and kept an eye out for the thugs. Although he'd detected the smooth growl of a finely tuned engine behind them, the twisting road and dense forest had prevented him from identifying its source. It certainly couldn't be the thugs. That wouldn't make sense.

"The oar might come in handy if the goons drop by," Dunky explained as they entered the dilapidated cottage.

Tony paused as a car drove slowly along the main road. Through the trees he glimpsed a passing black shadow. It didn't stop.

Quietly April breathed a sigh of relief. "You don't have to worry about the thugs," she told Dunky confidently. "Your bookie has been paid in full."

He squealed and enveloped them both in a brief, squeezing hug. Tony grinned and bore it. "I can go home, I can go home," Dunky chortled, clapping his hands. He reached for the slightly dented bakery box. "This calls for a celebration. Éclairs for everyone!"

"First things first. Where are the Fogbottoms?" Tony asked.

Dunky waved an unconcerned hand. "One's in the clothes hamper. The other's . . . oh, where did I put it? Under the sofa, I think."

April went to the bathroom and pulled the unframed fake Fogbottom out from under a pile of threadbare towels. Tony kneeled by the sofa and felt through the clumps of dust for the real thing. He was carefully slid ing it out when the suspicious sports car pulled into the driveway.

"Not the thugs," April cried, but she quickly knelt at the sofa and slid Dunky's forgery out of sight. Outside, a car door thunked.

Tony still held the genuine Fogbottom, gray threads of dust clinging to the carving of its heavy gilt frame. "Who do you know who drives a black sports car?"

Dunky crept into the living room area and stood cowering behind Tony, dangling the bakery box by its string from his crooked index finger. "Talon drives a Raptor."

April and Tony looked at each other, wary, but not really alarmed. "Talon," he said. "We forgot about Talon."

She burst into the room without knocking. Dunky jumped; the box of éclairs fell from his limp finger and landed upside down on the sofa. "Cripes, Talon, you scared me," he whined.

Dressed in a zippered black silk jumpsuit that made her look like a Bond girl, she paused just inside the doorway, her ebony eyes slitted. "I've come for the Fogbottom."

"You can't have it," Tony said, moving to rise from his knees.

Talon slipped a slim pearl-handled pistol from her pocket. "Don't move," she snarled. The gun was aimed not at Tony but at the oil painting propped beside him. Still a little too close for comfort. "Or the painting gets it."

"But I thought you wanted the Fogbottom!" April blurted.

Talon's lips twisted in disdain. "I don't care what happens to the original." Although she shrugged eloquently, her aim remained steady. "Give me trouble and I shoot it. Do as I say and you can keep it. All I want is Dunky's copy."

"Then what's to prevent us from going to the police?" asked Tony. His mind was working rapidly, plotting out ways to maneuver the gun away from Talon while keeping April out of firing range. At this point, he couldn't have cared less about the Fogbottom, and Donkey would probably hit the floor in a dead faint, conveniently putting the bulky sofa between him and Talon.

"Would you rat out your good friend Dunky?" Talon said with a menacing chuckle. "If I go to jail, so does my baby brother. I don't think you want that to happen, do you, April?"

April had been sidling around the sofa to get closer to the long wooden oar Dunky had propped against the back of it. She froze. "No," she said in a strangled voice.

"I can't go to jail." Dunky shuddered. "Think of the decor! And the food!"

Realizing April's intention, Tony tried to distract Talon. "When did you hire the thugs?"

"He means the goons," said Dunky. "T-Bone and Eldridge."

Talon looked pleased. "I thought that was quite efficient of me. Since the bookie had sent them out to collect from Dunky anyway, I made arrangements that they should also report to me. They didn't care about the Fogbottom, but I did, so they were happy to kill two birds with one stone . . . so to speak."

"Kill?" Dunky's voice was barely a squeak.

"You're such a wimp," Talon complained. "If you'd simply gone through with the deal as we agreed, the goons would have been paid off by now!"

"Talon, you don't want to do this," April pleaded. She was now standing beside the oar, six feet to Talon's left. "Wouldn't it be easier to book a few shows of salable paintings at the gallery? You could turn a legitimate profit instead of trading in forgeries."

Talon's black bob swung silkily when she shook her head. "It's too late for that."

But Dunky nodded. "My paintings are popular—"

"Your paintings are bourgeois," his sister sneered. "Amateur Hour. Anyway, Father would never allow you to exhibit them. He's sending you back to business school—if you ever come home."

"I won't go. I'm an *artiste,* not a desk jockey!"

"Then you'll be kicked out of Windenhall. As will I, unless I can prove Galerie Diabolique is thriving." She tilted her head, squinting one eye as she sighted down the barrel of the pistol. The fleshy behind of Fogbottom's wading nude made an excellent target. "The quarter of a mil McNair's paying for the fake Fogbottom will more than balance my books. And April can hold on to the original, as long as it stays out of sight and she keeps her mouth shut."

"You'll be arrested even if April agrees to do as you say," Tony said with firm conviction.

"I don't think so." But there was a hint of doubt in Talon's voice.

Tony seized on it. "Nelson McNair is a police detective. He's working undercover for the Art Fraud Squad."

"You're lying," she snapped. "How could you know such a thing?"

"Tell her about Uncle Rocco, April."

April could barely cover up her own surprise at Tony's revelation. "Uh, it's true, Talon. Tony's uncle used to be a member of the Chicago police department. He knows Nelson McNair. In fact, they were partners. They were the cops who busted open the infamous billion-dollar Matisse scam—"

"Simply put," Tony said, putting a stop to April's wild extemporizing, "Detective McNair has been setting you up. If you sell him a fake Fogbottom, you and Donkey will both be arrested."

"Ooh, I don't feel so good..." His face tinged green, Dunky swayed in place for a second or two, then collapsed onto the sofa with a groan. The flimsy bakery box, squashed flat beneath him, oozed éclair goo.

His sudden collapse distracted Talon. She jerked her head around, her grip tightening on the pistol so it flinched from its target. April snatched up the oar, swinging it overhead. Tony shot to his feet. He plunged toward Talon, kicking the Fogbottom out of the way.

She swiveled back toward him, her finger twitching on the trigger as she brought her other arm up to steady her aim. The blade of April's oar whistled through the air and struck Talon's forearm, knocking the gun out of her hand as it fired.

Tony went down.

April screamed. She flung herself over Talon's slumped form and dropped to her knees beside Tony. He was flat on his back, the Fogbottom laid across his chest. A scorch-edged bullet hole had pierced the center of the canvas.

"Oh, no, Tony, please, no..." Tears welled in April's eyes. They began to spill over as she lifted the painting off his chest with hands gone numb. He mumbled something indistinguishable. Sobbing, she threw the Fogbottom aside.

Expecting to see a fatal red stain blossoming across the front of Tony's shirt, April steeled herself. There was nothing. Crying even harder, she swiped at her eyes to look again. More tears immediately sprang forth and she peered through their blur, batting her lashes ineffectually. She saw no blood, no wound, only the rapid rise and fall of Tony's chest as he gasped for breath.

"You're still alive!" she cried through another bountiful gush of tears.

"Of course I'm alive," he panted, pushing himself up on his elbows.

April dived at him, knocking him flat again. She wound her arms around him and hugged his face to her abdomen so tightly he couldn't breathe. Through a white-hot burn of pain, he felt her body shudder with great, gasping sobs.

She sat up, pulling as much of him as possible into her lap. "You didn't get killed," she crooned through the waterfall of tears. They ran down her face and dripped onto his. "You didn't even get shot."

Wincing, he shifted out of her embrace. "I didn't exactly say *that*."

"But—" April stiffened, her eyes flooding with another fresh gust. Frantically weeping and moaning, she ran her palms over his crumpled body. "Oh, no, you've been shot, you've been shot," she babbled. "Where is the bullet? Where does it hurt? Dunky, call 911!"

"There's no phone," Dunky said dully from the couch, his hands sticky with the mushy remains of the éclairs.

"What about me?" Talon wailed. She was sprawled on the floor, cradling her arm to her chest. "I think you broke my arm."

"Well, you shot Tony!" April howled, her eyes wild.

Tony stared up into them, noticing something odd. Maybe the pain coursing up his leg was making him see things. "Your eyes," he said wonderingly. Tears, of such an abundance he began to think about arks, were cascading down her stricken face. "They're two different colors."

April rubbed them. "Never mind my eyes." She choked. "You've been shot."

"Only in the toe," he said.

She looked at his foot. A red blot stained the toe of his white sneakers. "Your toe?" she repeated, and snuffled noisily. Talon moaned in the background.

"Hurts like hell, though."

"Oh, poor Tony," April said, helping him sit up. She kissed his face wetly, wrapped her arms around him and rocked him like a baby. Tears—the physical release of her pent-up emotions—continued to flow; she felt as though she were careening pell-mell down a water slide, unable to stop, not even sure she wanted to. "I love you, Tony, poor Tony, darling Tony..."

"Please don't call me 'poor Tony,'" he mumbled. "But I wouldn't mind hearing that first part again."

"I love you," she said through her sobs. "I love you so much I'm never letting you get away from me. You're going to South America and I'm going to follow you, whether you like it or not." She took a deep, ratcheting breath. "*Someone* has to take care of you!"

"It appears that way," he said with a strained grin, "since this is yet another time you've come to my rescue." He kissed her lips, her cheeks, tasting the salty wetness of her tears. "April, my guardian angel."

"I love you."

"Mmm, balm for my injuries. Say it again."

"I love you." She started to laugh even though she was still crying. Her heart was bursting. "I love you."

"Then why are you crying?" he asked softly, holding her face in his hands, his thumbs wiping at the paths of her trickling tears.

"Because I love you." She made an odd sound, a breathy gulp. "I didn't cry for Freeman. I couldn't."

"Never?"

She shook her head. "He killed whatever love I might've once had for him. And that made me doubt I'd ever be able to love anyone again." She looked down, her spiky lashes fluttering against her damp pink cheeks, then stared straight into his eyes. "Until you, Tony. I do love you, so much. So very, very much."

"April," he whispered, holding her close. "I love you, too, but I think..." He planted another quick kiss on her soft, trembling lips. "You aren't crying only over me getting shot. I think maybe you're also finally crying for Freeman."

Could that be? She leaned her forehead against Tony's strong shoulder. It was true that although she felt sodden and heavy with the weight of her tears, there was also a sense of something different inside. Her heart was full but light; her conscience was clear. Freeman Pierce had been mourned at last. Now he was gone—washed away in the flood of long overdue tears.

She'd finally said goodbye.

"But I'll never let *you* go, Tony," she whispered. "Never."

He seemed to understand. "I promise you this, April, my love. It works both ways."

She looked up, her mismatched eyes brimming with tears of another kind. Tony recognized them.

They were tears of joy.

MUCH LATER, at the hospital, they straightened things out with the law, more or less explaining away the incident as an accidental mishap. Dunky had pleaded for leniency and none of them believed that Talon had actually intended to kill Tony. Finally, April and Tony managed to steal a moment alone together. They were in an examining room and the nurse had just left to get a few pain pills for Tony before discharging him. His big toe had only been nicked by Talon's off-course bullet. All the wound had required was cleansing and a bandage. Talon, however, was in X ray with a compound fracture of the ulna and a potential charge of reckless use of a firearm.

"Hazel," said Tony.

April blinked. "What?"

"Your eyes—they're hazel. A perfectly nice shade of hazel."

She wrinkled her nose. "Boring, you mean." She'd always thought her eyes were nondescript—a little green, a little brown, a little blah. She slipped the remaining tinted contact from her right eyeball and displayed the brown disc on the tip of her finger. "I guess the other one was washed away by all that crying."

Tony smiled. "Your eyes aren't boring. They're beautiful."

"Does this mean I have to give up my contacts?"

"They might be too bothersome in the jungle."

April's face glowed with hope as she turned back to Tony. "Do you mean it's okay if I—"

Dunky stuck his orange head inside the doorway. "Lucky thing about the Fogbottom!" he trumpeted.

"You and Talon owe April a masterpiece," Tony said. "And I don't mean a replica, either."

"But that's just it." Dunky bounded into the room. "Talon shot the wrong painting."

"I'm afraid you're the one who's wrong, Dunky," April lamented. "She shot the original. The one in the frame."

He scuffed his toe bashfully. "I was only trying it out to see how it looked . . ."

Tony added two and two. "Do you mean to say you'd taken the frame off the original and put it on the forgery?"

"The replica, yes."

Surprised and delighted, April clapped one palm to her forehead. "Then the real Fogbottom is still under the sofa!" she exclaimed, and threw her arms around Dunky. She kissed his cheek. "How brilliant of you, Dunks."

Tony rolled his eyes. "There you go, rewarding the wrong guy again."

She hugged Tony, too, gazing into his eyes with adoration. "You're both my heroes."

"Just one question," Dunky said. "Was that true about Nelson McNair being a cop?"

April was also curious. "Was it, Tony?"

He shrugged, his dimple deepening. "Rocco wouldn't know an art fraud if one shot him in the toe."

"Whew," Dunky said, playfully wiping his brow. "But that was still too close a call for me. My delicate constitution can't take these nerve-racking upsets."

"So please tell us that you've learned your lesson," April said. "Quit gambling. Never again pervert your artistic gift by painting forgeries. Please."

Dunky struck a tragic pose. "I'm giving it all up," he intoned sorrowfully—then couldn't hold back his glee. "Because guess what? I've managed to talk Talon into giving me a one-man show at her gallery. Only Darryl Dunkington originals," he added when he saw the look in Tony's eyes.

"What will your father say?" April asked.

He shrugged. "The show will just have to be a smashing success. The only thing MacArthur respects is money."

"I'll buy the first painting, Dunky," Tony promised.

"You will?"

"You called him *Dunky,*" April said in awe.

Tony grinned. "Just make sure it doesn't look anything like the Fogbottom."

Dunky clapped his hands. "Fabulous! Perhaps I'll paint you a nude portrait of April as a wedding present," he called over his shoulder as he flew out of the room. "*Ta-ta!* I've got to get Talon's signature on a letter of agreement while she's still woozy!"

They watched the door until it stopped swinging. Then Tony turned slowly to April. "So what about it?"

She wouldn't meet his eyes. "I might still qualify as an heiress, but I'm no longer that madcap. I think I'll be keeping my clothes on."

"Even on our honeymoon?"

She blushed. "Well, honeymoons are a different matter altogether..."

Tony, still sitting on the edge of the examining table, one shoe on and one shoe off, slid his hands around her waist and pulled her over so she was standing between his thighs. April sparkled with the thrill of his touch, her hazel eyes alight with emotion as she met his gaze. She'd thought that spending the last of the madcap money was what would heal her heart. Although it had helped, what had meant so much more was learning how to love...and accepting *being* loved by a man like Tony Farentino. It was the sort of lesson that would last a lifetime.

"The only way you're coming to Cayaxechun is as my bride," Tony vowed as the door silently swung open.

She kissed him. He kissed her. The nurse backed out of the room.

"The thing is," she said after a while, cuddled snugly in Tony's arms, "even though The Madcap Heiress spent all my ready cash, I still have an income from the Throckmorton trust fund. And I'll come into even more when I turn thirty. So..."

"So?" he asked warily.

"Do you see any reason why I can't use some of it to import a few luxuries to Guatemala? Say, fresh supplies of champagne and chocolates dropped off by helicopter? Maybe we could FedEx my bed from Chicago—I do adore that bed. And how much trouble could it be to ship in a few air conditioners...?"

Tony started to laugh.

"I suppose a swimming pool would be too extravagant," April added with a mischievous smile, thinking that there was plenty of time to tell Tony she wasn't kidding.

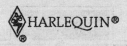
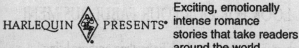

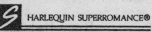

LOOK FOR OUR FOUR FABULOUS MEN!

Each month some of today's bestselling authors bring
four new fabulous men to Harlequin American Romance.
Whether they're rebel ranchers, millionaire power brokers
or sexy single dads, they're all gallant princes—and
they're all ready to sweep you into lighthearted fantasies
and contemporary fairy tales where anything is possible
and where all your dreams come true!

You don't even have to make a wish...Harlequin American
Romance will grant your every desire!

Look for Harlequin American Romance wherever Harlequin
books are sold!

Harlequin® Historical

If you're a serious fan of historical romance,
then you're in luck!

Harlequin Historicals brings you
stories by bestselling authors, rising new stars
and talented first-timers.

Ruth Langan & Theresa Michaels
Mary McBride & Cheryl St.John
Margaret Moore & Merline Lovelace
Julie Tetel & Nina Beaumont
Susan Amarillas & Ana Seymour
Deborah Simmons & Linda Castle
Cassandra Austin & Emily French
Miranda Jarrett & Suzanne Barclay
DeLoras Scott & Laurie Grant…

You'll never run out of favorites.

Harlequin Historicals…they're too good to miss!

HARLEQUIN  PRESENTS®

HARLEQUIN PRESENTS
men you won't be able to resist falling in love with...

HARLEQUIN PRESENTS
women who have feelings just like your own...

HARLEQUIN PRESENTS
powerful passion in exotic international settings...

HARLEQUIN PRESENTS
intense, dramatic stories that will keep you turning
to the very last page...

HARLEQUIN PRESENTS
The world's bestselling romance series!

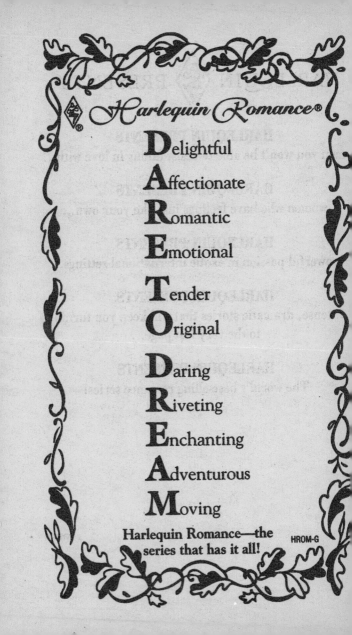

Harlequin Romance®

Delightful

Affectionate

Romantic

Emotional

Tender

Original

Daring

Riveting

Enchanting

Adventurous

Moving

Harlequin Romance—the
series that has it all!

HROM-G